TOP Ｓ
FOR YOUＲ

SUBJECT: Rod Gallowglass, aka Rodney d'Armand, SCENT agent

HISTORY: First hit *Escape Velocity* to leave home asteroid, and family cybernetics business. Agent landed on Gramarye, to aid establishment of a democratic government. Only companion: "Fess," an artificial intelligence disguised as a horse.

ANALYSIS: Went native. Became *The Warlock in Spite of Himself*, seeking his fame and fortune in this backwater world. Was instrumental, during the invasion of *King Kobold Revived*, in fulfilling his original mission of bringing democratic principles to a feudal society.

MISSION REFERENCE: See files *The Warlock Unlocked*, *The Warlock Enraged*, *The Warlock Wandering*, *The Warlock Is Missing*, *The Warlock Heretical*, *The Warlock's Companion*, *The Warlock Insane*, *The Warlock Rock*.

PROJECTION: Second-generation Warlock's family now coming of age. The children all possess psychic talents, or magical powers, as they're quaintly called on Gramarye. All four proving to be as trouble-prone as their parents—especially Magnus, the eldest son. For most recent missions, see *Warlock and Son*, and *A Wizard in Absentia*.

Ace Books by Christopher Stasheff

A WIZARD IN BEDLAM

The Warlock Series

ESCAPE VELOCITY
THE WARLOCK IN SPITE OF HIMSELF
KING KOBOLD REVIVED
THE WARLOCK UNLOCKED
THE WARLOCK ENRAGED
THE WARLOCK WANDERING
THE WARLOCK IS MISSING
THE WARLOCK HERETICAL
THE WARLOCK'S COMPANION
THE WARLOCK INSANE
THE WARLOCK ROCK
WARLOCK AND SON

A WIZARD IN ABSENTIA

A Wizard in Absentia

CHRISTOPHER STASHEFF

ACE BOOKS, NEW YORK

This book is an Ace original edition,
and has never been previously published.

A WIZARD IN ABSENTIA

An Ace Book / published by arrangement with
the author

PRINTING HISTORY
Ace edition / March 1993

All rights reserved.
Copyright © 1993 by Christopher Stasheff
Cover art by Ciruelo Cabral.
This book may not be reproduced in whole or in part,
by mimeograph or any other means, without permission.
For information address: The Berkley Publishing Group,
200 Madison Avenue, New York, NY 10016.

ISBN: 0-441-51569-X

Ace Books are published by The Berkley Publishing Group,
200 Madison Avenue, New York, NY 10016.
The name "ACE" and the "A" logo
are trademarks belonging to Charter Communications, Inc.

PRINTED IN THE UNITED STATES OF AMERICA

10 9 8 7 6 5 4 3 2 1

A Wizard in Absentia

CHAPTER
~1~

By the time the sun had risen, Ian had made perhaps three miles. Then, as the first rays touched him, he looked about for a hiding place. A thicket of young fir trees caught his eye, their branches sweeping down to the ground. He went to them and thrust his way between the branches into the brown circle about the trunk.

A man dressed in a green tunic and brown leggings leaned upon his spear, scowling thoughtfully.

Ian froze and caught his breath. A gamekeeper, and one who had no doubt been told to look for a run-away boy!

The keeper sighed, looked up—and saw Ian.

For a moment, they both stood stock-still, staring at one another. Then the keeper's face hardened and he came toward Ian, his hand outstretched.

Ian turned and bolted.

1

Behind him, he heard the keeper shout, heard his heavy feet pounding, and ran for his life.

A thicket loomed up before him. Without slackening his stride, he set the heel of his staff against the ground in front of the bushes and leaped. He swung up on the staff and over, like a clock's pendulum inverted. He shoved hard, and landed on the far side of the bushes. He stumbled and ran on, as fast as he could. Behind him, he heard the keeper cursing as he floundered through the bushes. He had bought a little time. Ian ran, zigzagging between the trees, around trunks. Taking a lesson from the dwarves, he chose trees with low branches that he could duck under, too low for the keeper to follow. Then two trunks appeared, so closely together that there was scarcely room for him to pass. He scrambled between them, but the keeper could not; that would slow him a little, too. His heart began to hammer; he could not seem to get enough breath. Gasping, he forced himself to run on, until suddenly the forest fell away and he was in a meadow, a clearing in the forest, with no place to hide. But a great round rock with a glint of metal to it stood up in the center of the meadow. The Stone Egg!

Ian turned to run back, but heard the keeper crashing through the underbrush behind him. He whirled again and ran towards the great stone egg, swerved around to its far side and crouched down, heart hammering, drawing in quick, deep breaths through his open mouth. Perhaps the keeper wouldn't see him, would think he had run back into the forest, or had run across the clearing and into the trees on the other side. Perhaps the keeper himself would plunge on across the grass, and not look back. . . .

But the keeper called out, and was answered by another shout from the far side of the clearing behind Ian. Another keeper!

Ian shrank back, gathering himself into a ball, pressing against the lower curve of the boulder, trying to press himself into the stone. . . .

Something clicked.

The surface behind him gave way, and Ian felt himself tumbling, saw a flash of light, then sudden darkness.

Two months earlier in time, and twenty light-years away in space, a very unusual asteroid drifted through the asteroid belt around Sol. It didn't look unusual—it seemed to be just an ordinary, everyday piece of space junk: lumpy, irregular, a few craters, a lot of raw rock, a lot bigger than most, a lot smaller than some—but all in all, nothing special, comparatively speaking. And comparisons were very easy to make at the moment, because it was in with a lot of others of its kind. In fact, you wouldn't have noticed it at all, if its trajectory hadn't been so different from those around it. They were moving placidly in orbit, just drifting along in their timeless round; but it was barreling straight toward one of the larger asteroids in the Belt—dodging and weaving around all the other asteroids, and no doubt taking a lot of hits from the pebble-sized junk, but still coming remorselessly toward Maxima. You just couldn't help noticing.

Especially if you were the Space Traffic Control

Center on that huge asteroid. "Unknown spacecraft! Identify yourself and sheer off! Maxima Control to unknown spaecraft! Identify yourself!"

"There is no reason not to, Magnus," the calm voice of the asteroid's computer said to its pilot—well, passenger, really; the *computer* was the pilot.

"I agree," said the tall, lantern-jawed young man. His eyes never flickered from the viewscreen as he watched the worldlet of his forefathers expand into a discernible disk, larger than all other space-sparks around it. "Identify us, Fess, and tell them we wish to land."

The robot tactfully refrained from telling his aristocratic young master that one did not merely inform Space Control that one was landing, and noted that he would have to explain a few customs to his young charge at the first opportunity. After all, a nobleman could not expect to give orders or pull rank when he was landing on a worldlet on which everybody was an aristocrat. "Spacecraft *FCC 651919*, under the auspices of the Society for the Conversion of Extraterrestrial Nascent Totalitarianisms, calling Maxima Control."

There was a moment of shocked silence at the other end of the link. Then the loudspeaker said, "Maxima Control here. How can we assist you, *FCC 651919*?"

"We request permission to land, Maxima Control."

"Permission . . . very good, *FCC 651919*. Searching for a landing slot for you. What is your cargo?"

"Supercargo only," said Fess, "Sir Magnus d'Armand, Lord Gallowglass."

Magnus stirred uncomfortably. "I am not yet a lord, Fess."

"You are the heir to the Lord High Warlock of Gramarye, Magnus," Fess reminded him sternly.

"Yet I have not been awarded any title of mine own."

"No doubt an oversight," Fess replied with airy disregard. "I am certain King Tuan would have given you an official title, for the asking."

Magnus smiled. "A lord without lands?"

"Certainly analogous to a minister without portfolio," Fess assured him. "Since your father is the equivalent of a duke, it follows that you must be the equivalent of a marquis—and in any event, you must have a title of some sort, if you wish to be treated with even a modicum of respect by the inhabitants of your ancestral home."

Maxima Control recovered from shock long enough to say, "Landing at 1030 hours Terran Standard, pad 29, berth 7-A. Approach from Galactic Northwest, declination 38 degrees 22 minutes, right ascension 21 degrees 17 minutes." Then a different voice spoke, feminine and mature. "Requesting permission to speak with your principal."

The lady was uncertain as to Magnus's status relative to Fess, the young man noted—was he owner, passenger, or captive? He leaned toward the audio pickup. Fess said quickly, "Remember, Magnus, to speak in modern English, and to avoid the second person singular."

5

"Yes, yes, I know," Magnus said testily, though it would be difficult to catch the knack of speaking without the *thees* and *thous* with which he had grown up. He smoothed his voice, keyed the pickup, and said, "Magnus d'Armand speaking." The name felt strange on his tongue—all his life he had been "Magnus Gallowglass," the patronymic his father had adopted as an alias when he landed on the psi-filled planet of Gramarye. But Magnus remembered his manners. "Good day to you, Maxima Control."

"And to yourself, my lord." The voice kept its punctilious politeness; Magnus may have only imagined the aura of amazement about it. "May I know your relationship to the family d'Armand?"

Magnus frowned.

"Relationships are extremely important to the Maximans, Magnus," Fess informed him, muting the audio pickup for the moment. "They must know your rank and place, if they are to know how to treat you."

The very notion rankled in a lad who had been reared to treat everyone with courtesy, but he was the scion of a medieval society, after all, so he could understand the need. "I am the son of Rodney d'Armand, who was a grandson of Count Rory d'Armand, and is a nephew of the current Count." At least, he hoped his great-uncle was still alive.

He was. "We shall inform his lordship that his great-nephew is landing," Maxima Control said, with a hint of reproach in her tone.

Magnus took it in stride. "I would appreciate the courtesy. I sent a message a week ago by hyper-radio, but I could not at that time give them an exact date of arrival."

"We understand." The voice seemed to thaw a bit. "How has Rodney Gallowglass come into possession of a title?"

Magnus stiffened. "In recognition of his services to the Crown of an interdicted colony, which he entered in his role as an agent of SCENT. You understand that any information more specific than that is also interdicted for protection of that colony, and may not be spoken publicly."

"I understand." But by its tone, the owner didn't. "Surely you can notify the head of the family of Rodney's . . . excuse me, Lord Rodney . . . of his location."

She wasn't sure the title was legitimate, Magnus noted. "Certainly," he said. "As head of a major corporation, he is cleared for secure knowledge, is he not?"

"He is. May I request visual contact?"

"At once! My apologies. Fess . . ." But before he could say, "if you please," a smaller screen suddenly came to life, filled with the picture of an imposing woman, imperially slim, with coiffured iron-gray hair and a face that was a tribute to the cosmetician's art. "I am your great-aunt Matilda, nephew Magnus. Welcome to Maxima."

Fess explained it on the way down—the robots took care of all the routine chores, such as traffic control, but when an unusual situation arose, requiring human judgement, the traffic computer would refer the matter to whichever human being happened to be on duty that day—and since everyone on Maxima claimed to be an aristocrat, it followed that even a countess had to take her shift at supervision.

Besides, it lightened the boredom.

There was a great deal of boredom on Maxima, as Magnus quickly found out. Everyone thought of himself or herself as an aristocrat, and consequently did very little work. Of course, their ancestors had been commoners, though outstanding ones—scientists, manufacturers, and businessmen, and many had been combinations of all three. They had come to Maxima for the freedom to do basic research into artificial intelligence and cybernetics without the interference of the Terran government (which became more and more restrictive as the Proletarian Eclectic State of Terra took hold more and more firmly), or to apply that research to making bigger and better robots. To support themselves, they went into manufacturing, and quickly gained a reputation for making the best robots in the Terran Sphere. Some of the sons who matured about that time had a bent for business, and by the second generation, every family on Maxima was wealthy. Since they lived like lords, they decided they should *be* lords, and in their legislative assembly, started ennobling each other at a startling rate. Since they were a sovereign government, even the Terran College of Heralds couldn't deny the technical legality of it, though they could certainly cast a skeptical glance.

On the other hand, many of the noble houses of Terra had had similarly disreputable founders.

After five hundred years of learning aristocratic ways, though, the Maximans had become nobility so thoroughly as to be indistinguishable from the old Terran families, in behavior if not in lineage. The more energetic of the sons ran the family businesses, thereby giving the lie to their pretended nobility, though they maintained the façade of leaving the business to their robots; they merely amused themselves by setting policy. Those activities couldn't absorb more than a handful, though, so some of the best and brightest began to emigrate to other planets—and as the centuries rolled by and the businesses came inevitably into the hands of the eldest sons, the brain drain increased. Additionally, Maximans tended to marry Maximans, even after they had all become cousins of one another, and the inbreeding took its toll.

Magnus's father, Rod, had been one of the energetic ones, as well as one of the brighter souls thrown up by inbreeding—and if he wasn't completely stable, well, who was? In any event, he had also become part of the brain drain, leaving Maxima for a career of high adventure and low income. Being the second son of a second son had had something to do with it, but so had boredom.

Which may also have had something to do with Magnus's feeling like a canary invited to a cats' party, as he stepped out of the airlock of his ancestral mansion to find himself confronted with a milling mob of richly dressed people, loud with excited conversation—which stopped abruptly as they realized he was there, and all eyes turned to him. Magnus felt like bolting right back into the boarding tunnel, but he remembered that he came of a warrior sire, and stiffened his spine, drawing himself up to his full height. He was much taller than the norm. He was, he knew, an impressive figure, and he smiled slightly at the reaction of the crowd.

Aunt Matilda stepped forward—or the Countess d'Armand, Magnus reminded himself—and said, "Welcome to Castle d'Armand, nephew Magnus."

Magnus suppressed the jolt of surprise he felt at the term "castle"—this glittering assemblage of baroque and rococo towers and arches might have been a palace, but certainly not a castle—and inclined his head politely. "Thank you, Countess."

It was the right choice; she smiled, pleased, but assured him, " 'Aunt Matilda,' nephew—we are all family here."

That was true enough, Magnus reflected—for the whole asteroid, not just Castle d'Armand.

"Your relatives." Matilda gestured toward the mob behind her, and one buxom, blonde vision pushed forward, eyes alight with curiosity and eagerness, reminding Magnus that he was probably the biggest event to happen all year—anything to break the monotony. The Countess tried to give the girl a frown of displeasure, but she couldn't sustain it. "My youngest granddaughter, Pelisse."

The lady stepped forward, extending her hand. Magnus bowed his head and pressed Pelisse's fingers briefly to his lips, trying to adjust to the notion of his uncle's youngest being nearly of an age with him, the eldest of Rod's children—but Uncle Richard was older than Rod by a few years, and had no doubt begun his family at a younger age.

Then Magnus looked up into the largest pair of sky-blue eyes he had ever seen, framed by a wealth of blonde hair so light as to be almost white, and froze, feeling as though he'd been filled with a humming energy, and as though his brain were not quite within his skull any longer. Desperately, he reminded himself that she was his first cousin, and that helped—but his hackles were still raised.

"I shall look forward to your closer acquaintance, cousin," she said, with amusement in her heavy-lidded glance, and the Countess cleared her throat. Pelisse made a *moue* and stepped back. Aunt Matilda said, "Your cousin Rath," and a long, lean individual stepped forward to give Magnus a perfunctory bow, and a look of morose hostility.

It helped bring Magnus back to the reality of the situation. He returned the bow stiffly, and Aunt Matilda said, "Your cousin Robert . . ."

Inwardly, Magnus sighed, and braced himself for a long session of bowing and kissing hands.

A long half-hour later, he straightened up from greeting the last relative, and turned to Aunt Matilda with a frown—which he quickly removed. *Fess, I've not met the Count!*

It would be impolitic to ask why, Fess replied, broadcasting on the frequency of human thought, but in the encoded mode of the Gallowglass family. *You may, however, request permission to greet him.*

"This has been a most excellent pleasure, milady,"

11

Magnus said. "However, I would also be pleased to greet my great-uncle, if I may."

"Of course, dear boy—yet surely you must have some refreshment first." Matilda glided over to him, hooking a hand through his elbow and using it to steer him through the mob of cousins. "You must be quite wearied from your travels, if not from your arrival. A glass of wine and a little nourishment will restore your strength."

Magnus followed, wondering why she was stalling—or did he really need to be fortified to greet the Count?

He did.

Count Rupert sat in bed, propped up by a half-dozen pillows. His hair was white, his face drawn and lined. Magnus stared, then covered the gaffe with a bow—surely they were mistaken! Surely this ancient was his great-grandfather, not his great-uncle! *Fess, he is aged immensely, and so fragile that a breath might blow him away!*

"Courteous," the invalid croaked, in a voice that still had some echo of authority, "but impetuous. I am not a king, boy—you need not bow at the door. Come closer to me."

Magnus obeyed without speech, for he was listening to Fess advising him, *Do not inquire as to the nature of the disease, Magnus. We will no doubt learn of it later.*

Magnus stepped up to the bedside, and the Count looked him up and down with a rheumy eye. "Your garb is quaint. They tell me you have come from a distant planet."

"Aye, sir—one where your nephew, my father, has made a place for himself."

"And you have left him?" the old man said with a touch of sarcasm. "Well, I am accustomed to that." He frowned up at Magnus, who was still trying to digest the shock of his words. "You have turned out well, young man—tall, and broad. And there is something of your father in your looks—strong features, let us say—but so much broader, so much heavier!"

The first part surprised Magnus; he had never heard anyone comment on his resemblance to his father—nor to his mother—since he had changed from child to young man. As to the second . . . "The bulk is the gift of my mother's father, milord." Which was true, proportionally; there was no need to mention that his maternal grandfather, Brom O'Berin, was scarcely three feet tall, though stocky as a bull.

"Yes, your mother." The old man frowned—almost painfully, as though even moving his face cost him great energy. "What is she? How did my nephew marry?" Before Magnus could answer, he waved away the reply. "Oh yes, I know that every mother appears as an angel to her son—and she must be a wonder, to hold Rodney together long enough for him to stay till you grew. But what is she like? Tell me the externals!"

"Well . . ." Magnus collected his wits; it had been a startling view of his father, though one he could believe. "She is the daughter of a king, milord." He didn't think he needed to mention that Brom

13

O'Berin was the King of the Elves—or that Gwen didn't know he was her father.

"A princess!" The Count stared, round-eyed. "Then he is a king—or will be?"

"No, my lord . . ." How could he phrase this?

Her line does not reign, Magnus.

"No," Magnus went on, with relief, "for her line will not reign."

"A cadet branch." The count nodded. "Then he will be a duke."

"Its equivalent, my lord, for he has won his own title by service to the reigning monarch."

"What title is that?" the Countess asked.

Magnus swallowed and took the plunge. "Lord High Warlock."

"Odd." The Count took it without batting an eye. "But *autre temps, autre moeurs.* Each culture has its own *Weltanschauung,* its own world-view, and its own titles. If he is the High Warlock, then you, no doubt, are only Lord Warlock?"

Magnus stood a moment, staring.

Say yes, Magnus.

"Why . . . quite so! How perceptive of you, milord."

"It is only reason." The old man was obviously pleased by the flattery. "And how does my nephew?"

"He is in good health, milord." A shadow crossed the Count's face, and Magnus hastened to add, "At least, at the moment."

"Ah." The Count nodded. "His old malaise, eh?"

"I . . . cannot say," Magnus floundered. "He has not spoken of it."

"His mind, boy, his mind!" the old man said impatiently. "The family's mental instability! Though he showed it less than most—only in a bit of paranoia, and a frantic need to leave the planetoid."

The second, Magnus was already beginning to understand, and he didn't think it had anything to do with mental illness. As to the first, however . . . "I regret to say that his paranoia has increased, my lord."

"Ah." The Count nodded, satisfied. "He has his good days, though, eh?"

"Yes, milord—and on one of them, he sent his best wishes to you, his uncle, and asked that I bring word of you."

"He shall have it, have a letter! Which shall tell him of my delight at his good fortune, and his accomplishments! I was sure he had been a credit to the family! But this planet he has made his home, young man—what of it, eh?" When Magnus hesitated, he said, "You may tell me—I am cleared for the highest level of security." He gestured impatiently at a waiting butler. "Show him the documents, Hiram."

"No, milord—'tis not necessary!" Magnus said quickly. "He hath come—uh, has come—to a Lost Colony, one named Gramarye. You . . . knew of his, ah, affiliation?"

"That he had become an agent of SCENT? Yes, yes," the old man said impatiently. "And this planet is their concern, eh?"

"Yes, my lord. It has regressed to a medieval culture"—actually, Magnus wasn't sure "regressed"

15

was the right word for something that had been done intentionally—"and is ruled by a monarchy. It is my father's intention to bring about the changes in their social and economic structure that will result in their evolving a form of democratic government."

"A huge undertaking, and a long one! How frustrating it must be, to commence a project that you will not live to see come to fruition, that even your children will not see finished! But is there progress, young man?"

"Some, my lord. There have been attempts to unseat the monarch in favor of warlords and dictators, but my father has held Their Majesties secure. . . ."

"As a nobleman should! But has he furthered a tyranny?"

"No, my lord, for he has built in systems for Their Majesties to take council from their lords." Magnus smiled. "In tr— In fact, he has managed to wring from each attempted *coup d'état* some change in government that plants yet one more seed of the democracy that will be."

The old man nodded. "Small wonder your monarch has elevated him to the peerage! You inherit, then, not only his title, but also his work! You are a double heir." The old man frowned. "Why are you here? Surely your place is by his side!" Again, he waved away Magnus's answer before it was made. "Oh, yes, I realize you must have your education—but you must return to him! You must!"

Magnus bridled, but even as his emotions surged, he remembered to analyze. Why did the Count feel so strongly on the issue? "As you say, my lord, I must have a modern education—I must absorb the current state of knowledge in the Terran Sphere, but even more, I must learn to deal with its men of power."

The old lord nodded slowly, his eyes narrowing. "Even so, even so! Rodney, of course, knows the ways of such dealings, having been reared and educated on Maxima, and tried in the crucible of government service—but you, too, must learn such ways, for you will have to represent your planet before the Sphere, will you not? Yes, of course you will!"

Magnus was glad the old man had answered his own question.

"We must see to his placement at Oxford," the Countess contributed.

"Or Harvard, or Heidelberg, eh? Yes, of course! My wife will make you acquainted with them, young man, and you may choose! And in the long vacations, we shall have to see to gaining visiting positions for you in commerce and government! Eh?"

"Your lordship is . . . too kind." Truthfully, Magnus was dazzled by their readiness to help—but he was also wary of it, perhaps because he wasn't all that certain that he wished to spend several years at a university. Fess had assured him that he had gained the equivalent in knowledge from the robot's tutelage. Still, it might be a good way to get the feel of this strange culture.

"Not at all, not at all!" The Count brushed aside the thanks, but seemed pleased anyway. It was hard to tell, of course—he spoke as though from an inexhaustible supply of energy, but his eyelids had begun to droop, he raised his hand as though it bore leaden

17

weights, and his shoulders slumped. Magnus searched for some way to end the interview and let the old man rest, but could think of none.

The Countess saved him. "We may begin that search now, husband. Or, perhaps, the young man should dress for dinner."

"Dinner?" The Count frowned. "Yes, Yes! I, too, I must . . ." He struggled to sit up, but the effort was too much for him. His wife stepped up to lay a gentle hand on his shoulder, and he sagged back against the pillows. "Perhaps in a little while. Yes? Only a little rest, now—then I'll dress. . . ."

"Quite right, husband. We will leave you, for the moment." She went toward the door, bending a severe glance on Magnus.

He bowed. "I thank you for this conversation, my lord, and for your hospitality."

"Not at all, not at all! Always good to have family come home, eh? But not so long, Rodney, not so long again, hm?" The Count seemed to diminish, to sink into the pillows, his eyes half-closing. "At supper, then."

"Of course, my lord." Magnus stepped away and moved quietly to the door. Aunt Matilda gave him a smile with a little genuine warmth in it, and beckoned him out the door. It closed behind him, as the nurse robot wheeled silently over to the Count.

Magnus's mind raced. He couldn't very well comment on the Count's frailty, or his surprise at it.

Matilda seemed to sense his quandary, and said, "He will not join us at dinner. He really must not leave his bed, except for short exercise walks with the nurses."

"Of course he must conserve his energies," Magnus agreed. "He is . . . a commanding presence." He had almost said "still," but had choked it back.

"In rare moments," the Countess said. "We try not to trouble him with major decisions just now."

Magnus took the hint. The Count was still head of the family—but in name only. He tried for a quick change of subject. "It has been an honor to meet the Count—but I must also pay my respects to my father's brother. May I see him?"

The Countess hesitated, her visage darkening, biting her lip. Magnus braced himself against apprehension. "He doth . . . does still live, does he not?"

"He does, yes," the Countess said reluctantly.

"And I may see him, may I not?"

"If it is one of his good days, yes."

Some hours later, Magnus returned, numbed, to the opulent guest room the robot-domo had assigned to him. He collapsed into an overstuffed chair, loosing his hold on his mind and letting it turn to the oatmeal it felt to be. After a long interval of silence, a voice spoke in his mind. *Magnus?*

Aye, Fess, he answered.

Are you well?

Magnus stirred. *Well enough. It hath been summat of a shock, though, to find that my uncle Richard is insane.*

I am sorry, Magnus, the robot-horse said, with something resembling a sigh—just "robot," Magnus reminded himself; Fess was the computer-brain for a spaceship now. But he still held the mental image of the horse body that Fess had worn for as long as Magnus had known him.

Sorry? For what?

I thought I had prepared you adequately for the insanity that has plagued the Gallowglass family for generations—all of Maxima, for that matter.

Magnus made a short, chopping gesture, though Fess couldn't see him. *You did all that you could, Fess. Nothing can truly prepare a body for the sight of a relative who has taken leave of his senses.*

Was he truly as bad as that?

Oh, not bad at all, in some ways—he doth seem to be happy, quite happy indeed. 'Tis simply that he doth know he is King Henry the Sixth reborn, and is quite content to wait in his monk's cell for the reincarnated Queen Margaret to release him.

Fess was silent for a moment, then said, *I grieve to hear it.*

Magnus laid his head back against the chair with a sigh. *At the least, he is not troubled or sunk in gloom.*

Yes, praise Heaven for that.

Oh, he doth! He doth thank Heaven for life, for food, for housing, for the flow of blood and the smallest worm that burrows 'neath the soil of Terra! He doth spend hours in prayer, and is sure of his sainthood to come!

It must be quite reassuring, Fess said slowly, *to have such confidence in the Afterlife.*

Magnus shuddered. *If that is religion, I'll none of it. Small wonder his son fled to Terra.*

Fled? Fess said, puzzled.

Magnus shrugged. *Gone to university, then, and become a scholar. Will you, nill you, he is set upon his professorship, and hath sent word that he will not return to Maxima.*

And has only the one daughter?

Aye, my cousin Pelisse, who doth play the co-quette with me. Magnus smiled in pleased reminis-cence. *I cannot be so pleasant to regard as all that, can I, Fess?*

You are quite imposing, Fess said slowly, *and your face has a certain rough-hewn comeliness.*

More to the point, I am someone new in her life, Magnus thought, amused. *Anyone from off-planet must be of greater interest than someone near, eh?*

No doubt an inborn reflex that evolved to mini-mize inbreeding, Fess mused. *Nonetheless, in the case of this stranger, the inbreeding would still ex-ist.*

Not wholly—I am only half of Maxima, Magnus thought absently, most of his mind given over to the contemplation of the lovely vision with blonde tresses and long lashes. He felt a quickening of interest—but also felt how superficial it was, how little real emotion it held. Had the witches of Gram-arye made him forever heartless?

Then he remembered the image of the golden box around his heart, given him by a Victorian ragpicker who must surely have been only a hallucination, a projection of his subconcious, an illusion that only a projective telepath such as Magnus himself could engender. He had accepted the gift, had locked his heart in a box of golden, and wondered if he could ever find the key.

Flirting is a harmless game, Magnus, Fess assured him, *as long as you remember it is only a game— and are sure the lady does, too.*

Aye, only a game, and great fun. Magnus pushed himself out of the chair, coming to his feet with a renewal of energy. *Let us resume the play, then.* And he turned away to the closet and the modern formal wear it held, to dress for dinner.

CHAPTER
~2~

A shout of pure terror rose to Ian's lips, but he bit
down on it, as much afraid of the keepers as of this
fall into the unknown.

There was a soft light about him, and his bottom
struck a yielding surface. He fell backwards head
over heels, then rolled and came up to his feet as his
father had taught him, looking about him in panic.
He was inside the Stone Egg!

Outside, the keepers must surely be looking for
him, calling to one another and running about—but
he heard nothing except a whisper of moving air, and
a faint hum, so faint that he felt it more than heard
it. It flashed through his mind that this must be a
safe place that the dwarves had built, but when he
looked more closely at his surroundings, he found
them completely strange, alien. Surely the dwarves
could never have grown this odd golden moss beneath his feet, the great chair that looked to be of

leather with a row of peculiar square windows in
front of it and a greater square above—but windows
that were blank and empty, showing only the gray of
the rock's surface. For a moment, Ian strained to
understand—what good was a window that showed
only the inside of a shell?

"Safety Base Forty-three ready to function as you
may command."

Ian hunched down into a ball, his staff raised to defend himself, looking about wildly—but he could
not see the person who had spoken.

The voice spoke again, deep and resonant, a man's
voice, though with a strange lack of feeling. "This fa-
cility is completely automated. Food and drink are
prepared from cryogenic stock. Armament is activated. Communications facilities are functional.
Safety Base Forty-three is at your disposal."

The voice was suddenly silent. Ian held himself
ready, looking about, waiting for it to speak again, to
demand he say what he was doing there. It was a rich
voice, a lord's voice. Surely it would demand to know
why a mere serf had invaded its hideaway. . . ?

The chamber was still; the voice was silent. No
one spoke, no one moved.

Slowly, Ian uncurled himself; more slowly still, he
stood up, looking about at the rich surroundings, his
pulse beginning to slow. The voice must be that of a
guardian spirit—for certainly, inside this egg, there
was scarcely room enough for two grown men. No
one could hide from him.

Except for the guardian spirit.

The flesh on his back crawled. He looked behind

him, and behind him again. There was no defense against a spirit. . . .

But it did not attack him, it did not seek to take vengeance. It had said it was preparing food and drink. If it sought to help him . . . Ian breathed more easily, and looked about him yet once more. He was safe for the moment; he could not have asked for a better hideaway until dark. What was this strange place he was in?

There was an air of quiet orderliness about him, of safety and security. Ian began to relax, studying the chamber in which he found himself. At the far side, there was a round black hole in the floor with a low guardrail about it. Ian went over to it and peered down. A flight of spiral steps led to a room below. How strange that there was light, a soft light coming from nowhere that he could find! He retreated from the hole; perhaps that was where the guardian spirit lived. Later he might go down there and see—but only if he was sure it was safe. For now, it would be better to leave it alone.

He looked at the great chair, went closer to it, inspecting it. If this was a sanctuary to protect anyone who needed it, then surely this chair was for him to sit in. He clambered up, sat down, and looked at the table in front of him. It was shallow, only as deep as his forearm, and set with little circles and bars that glowed in many different colors. Their soft light struck fear into him, but he plucked up his courage and dared to poise a finger over one of them. Then his boldness failed, and he snatched his finger away. No, certainly he should not meddle with such things!

But—why not? If the "Base" was here to protect him, would he not be free to do as he wished? Perhaps, though, if he pressed one of these glowing circlets, the spirit would be angered, and would seek to revenge itself on him.

"Food and drink are prepared."

Ian started at the suddenness of the deep voice, then caught himself with a hand against the table in front of him. . . .

Something clicked.

His gaze darted down; he stared in horror at the heel of his hand. Slowly, he lifted it away, and saw that one of the green circlets had sunk into the tabletop. A low humming began. He backed away against the chair, eyes wide. Had he angered the spirit?

One of the square windows before him suddenly filled with light. Ian thought he must be looking out into the middle of a blizzard; there were only flecks of black and white, chasing each other past the window. At the same time, he heard a hiss begin, and the guardian spirit spoke. "Communication system is activated. Beacon is broadcasting distress signal."

Then the voice was quiet. Ian waited, tensed, but nothing more happened. He looked down at the circlet. Should he try to pry it back up out of the tabletop?

No. The guardian spirit did not seem angered, and had not threatened to harm him. Better to leave well enough alone.

But the spirit spoke again. "Food and drink are served."

Ian looked up, heart hammering—but at last, the

words sank in. Food and drink! Suddenly, he was very hungry. But where were they? He searched all around the cabin, being careful not to touch anything. As he passed the hole with the spiral staircase, he caught the scent of fresh bread, eggs, and, wonder of wonders, pork! His mouth watered; he swallowed heavily, the hunger suddenly an ache in his belly. The food was down the spiral staircase, then. But was it safe to go down there? Or was the guardian spirit enticing him for some other, unknown purpose? He stood stock-still at the top of the steps, wondering. Then hunger got the better of caution, and he started down.

The staircase was steep and narrow, made out of some eldritch material that was neither stone nor metal nor wood, but something of all three—clean and smooth to the touch like metal, warm like wood, and gray like stone. It was just wide enough for a full-grown man, very steep, and turned upon itself like a corkscrew.

His eyes came below the level of the floor, and he stopped, staring in amazement.

Ten feet below him was a circle of the odd moss, wider than the hut in which he'd lived all his life. The walls sloped inward, like the inside of a cone with its top cut off. The "egg," then, was the top of this cone, and this chamber was underground!

The strange, warm moss covered another floor, and this time, that moss was deep blue. Great padded chairs stood near him, and across the room stood a round table with two stools that had backs rising up—why, they were lords' chairs! Trepidation rose in him all over again, fear at trespeassing in a place so clearly the property of some great lord—but hunger was greater than fear. Two chairs! Was there company, then? Or was it merely that this hiding place was large enough for two people at a time?

A lord's hideaway for a dalliance with a peasant wench!

But on the table was a plate with thin slices of meat and, wonder of wonders, a silver fork and spoon and knife beside it! He blinked, overawed by the luxury, and, very hesitantly and carefully, came to the table.

Nothing bad happened.

He slid up onto one of the lords' chairs and, ignoring the knife and fork, began to eat with his fingers. If they caught him here, at least they would not be able to say he had stolen—for surely, stealing such treasure as a silver fork would be cause for hanging a serf!

He ate like a wolf, and the food was gone very quickly. Then he huddled back in the chair, wishing there were more, and staring at the steaming cup in front of him. The meat had been salty, and his thirst grew as he stared at the cup. Finally, he reached out and lifted it by the little handle. It almost overbalanced and spilled, but he caught it in time; the fluid within it was very hot and a dark brown. He sipped at it and made a face. It was very bitter. How could a lord like such stuff? He set it down and, instead, picked up a glittering, clear cup filled with orange liquid, sipped it carefully, decided it was very good, and drank it down. Then he looked about him, frowning. Strange that the dwarves had not found this place. . . .

He shrugged. There was no point in wondering at it. He slid down from the chair. It was still daylight outside, and he could not go out again until night. How he would get out was another problem; but the spirit had been good to him so far, and he would worry about that difficulty when the time came. He stretched himself out on the moss—it was very soft—pillowed his head on his arm, and was very quickly asleep.

When Magnus entered the dining room in black complet and snowy shirtfront and neckcloth, Pelisse clapped her hands. "Oh! How handsome you look!"

Robert glared at her. "Overdoing it a bit, aren't we, Pelisse?"

"Oh, do be still, Robert! Even you must admit that he looks ever so elegant!"

"Yes, Robert, you must," Aunt Matilda said, with a glare.

"Well . . . a sight better than that outlandish outfit he was wearing this afternoon," Robert mumbled.

Magnus felt his face flush, and was all the more careful to hold his expression immobile. "Literally outlandish, of course, and quite medieval—just the sort of thing you would wear on my homeworld."

"Yes, but not in civilized society, is it, old boy?"

Magnus let the "old boy" pass. "Perhaps you mean *modern* society—though I do note that these garments tend much more toward the turn of the century."

"Turn of the century?" Robert looked up, frowning. "Stuff and nonsense! Lapels much wider then, don't you know, and trousers much looser!"

"I was speaking of the turn of the Eighteenth Century into the Nineteenth—the decade that began in 1810, as a matter of fact."

Robert could only glare at him, and Magnus realized, with a shock, that the young man probably knew nothing about the Eighteenth and Nineteenth Centuries, didn't know that the clothes he was wearing were very clearly based on those of the Regency.

Aunt Matilda filled the gap. "You must remember, children, that your cousin's garb was that of his own culture; it is our costumes that would look outlandish there."

"Like his *thee's* and *thou's*, eh?" Robert muttered.

Magnus felt his face flame again, and resolved to make no more slips.

"Yes, quite. Robert, perhaps tomorrow you will escort Magnus to the family tailor? And the haberdasher, of course."

Robert turned red, and his jaw set—but he ground out, "Yes, Aunt."

"Very good." Matilda favored them all with a bright smile. "Now, then, shall we dine?"

The robots began serving, and Magnus reflected on the lovely, charming family from which he had come.

He was braced for the shopping expedition with Cousin Robert the next day, and it was just as grueling as he had feared. Robert began with whining complaints and progressed to sniping comments very quickly. Magnus responded as politely as he could, but couldn't quite keep back a few remarks of his own.

For example, when the air-lock door dilated and Magnus found himself staring at the inside of a small but luxurious rocket boat, Robert snapped, "Don't look so surprised. You can't just walk where you please on an asteroid, you know. No air."

"Of course." Magnus stepped in and sat down. Robert followed suit, grumbling, "Don't know why Mama picked me for this little chore. Pelisse would have been more than happy to show you around."

"Whereas you, of course, are delighted."

"No, not a bit." Robert turned to frown at him. "Planned on a morning's practice at polo, actually. Where'd you get an idea like that?"

Magnus found himself wondering if Robert knew what the word "sarcasm" meant.

"Deuced inconvenience," Robert complained. "Why'd you have to come, anyway?"

Magnus ground his teeth and said, "To discover my origins, Cousin Robert—what kind of people I came from, what kind of environment had formed them."

"Had your father to look at, didn't you?"

"Indeed," Magnus agreed, "but one person is not necessarily representative of the whole family." *Thank Heaven*, he added silently to himself.

"Don't know why we have to have dashed outsiders," Robert went on as though he had not heard. "Doing quite well enough by ourselves."

Magnus began to wonder if the man knew he was speaking aloud.

"Bad enough trying to sort out the inheritance as it is," Robert griped. "Of course, Pelisse will take care of that—but still, it's a dashed nuisance."

Magnus gave him a sharp glance. "Inheritance? Why should that be a problem? Has someone died recently?"

"Not yet, y'—" Robert bit off the expletive, which was just as well, Magnus thought grimly. Then his cousin went on. "Death that's coming, of course. Uncle can't last much longer, more's the pity, and his son's made it very clear he doesn't want the inheritance. That leaves it to Pelisse, don't y' see."

"No, I don't." Magnus frowned. "Isn't your inheritance patrilineal?"

"What?" Robert gave him a narrow look. "Don't use your fancy terms on me, my man! Say what you mean in clear language, dash it all!"

Magnus was beginning to think that he had overrated Robert's intelligence, as well as his education. "Don't you inherit, as the remaining male?"

"No, I don't—I'm the poor relation. Don't you know anything?"

"Nothing more than I'm told," Magnus said shortly, "and I would thank you for doing so."

"Well, I'm a third cousin," Robert snapped, "from the Orlin branch—parents died young, and I was as close to this family as to t'other. So, no, I don't inherit, though I expect Uncle's left me well enough off. Have m' biological parents' estate coming, in any case, when I reach my majority."

"Majority?" The man was clearly in his twenties! Magnus decided not to ask—he just accepted the prevailing wisdom. "So Pelisse will become Countess," Magnus inferred.

"No reason not to," Robert muttered, but he gave Magnus an uneasy glance, leaving his guest wondering just how Pelisse was supposed to fix any problems arising from the inheritance. In fact, of course, Robert hadn't mentioned what the problem was, really. Somehow, Magnus thought he didn't want to know.

Their flier circled around a huge, pastel layer-cake of a building and docked. They stepped out into an air lock. As they walked down the tube and through the dilating door, Magnus said, "Surely you could have your own robot tailors, and order anything from outside by video screen."

"Of course, of course," Robert said impatiently, "but then there wouldn't be any shopping, hey? Nor any reason to get out of the house at all. Let's have a quick one, then get on to the tailor's."

Magnus was relieved to discover that Robert was referring to an alcoholic drink. He wasn't so relieved when the "quick one" turned into two or three.

The tailor was a robot, after all, and all he had to do to measure Magnus was to have him stand against a wall screen that did the job in less than a second. Then they sauntered down rows of fabrics, with Robert brightly extolling the virtues of each until Magnus selected a few, just to shut him up—he thought they were rather gaudy, himself, but they were Robert's recommendations. His cousin seemed to think

Magnus's preference for quieter fabrics was very unsophisticated.

"And have that delivered by 1700 hours," Robert told the robot tailor as they left.

It bowed. "As you wish, sir."

As they strolled out of the store, Magnus protested, "There was no reason for haste."

"'Course there was, old boy—the ball next week. Don't you remember?"

"I can't very well," Magnus said slowly, "since I haven't been told. What ball?"

"The one Mama is throwing! In your honor, old—I say! There's Runcible!" And he hurried off to chat with a chum.

Magnus observed the two, noting the degree of loudness, the social distance between them, the lack of physical touching, the intonations, and half-a-dozen other signs of modern customs—but all the time, at the back of his mind, he was wondering why his aunt was putting on an impromptu ball, and why it was in his honor. Were they that desperate for something to do, for some trace of excitement, here?

Yes. Of course they were. How could he ever have wondered?

The haberdasher's was only a hundred meters away, but it took them half an hour to get there—Robert had to stop every few feet to greet friends, and had to beg off coming to drink with them because he had to squire his bothersome cousin around—and he didn't hesitate to use those terms, when he must have known full well that Magnus could hear him. If he had thought of it. Magnus was beginning to wonder just how good a guide Robert was to the manners of this people.

He was very much aware of being the outsider, studying the customs as though he were an anthropologist, though for a much more pressing reason than academic research. It was horrifying to realize that this subject group he was observing were supposed to be his own flesh and blood, the people and stock from which he had sprung.

He understood now why his father had left home. In fact, he had gone beyond a mere understanding to a very active sympathy.

The haberdashery comprised a vast assortment of hats and ties and other accessories. They could all have been displayed on screens, of course, and the orders placed by computer— but that would have deprived the young men of a reason to go sauntering down the aisles, where they could be sure of encountering one another and pause for a good, long chat. Magnus resigned himself to a long and boring afternoon, the more so because he was seldom introduced and never included in the conversation—not that he would have wanted to be; it seemed to be exclusively a discussion of the latest styles, sports averages, and local scandals about who was sleeping in whose bed. Magnus was sure it would have been fascinating, if he had only known what they were talking about.

So, when they arrived at home and he had endured high tea and was finally able to seek the comfort of his own rooms, he keyed the wall screen to news, and spent an hour absorbing a quick summary of recent events—local, Terran, and throughout the

Terran Sphere. Where he needed additional background to make sense of the summary, he keyed for more information—but still, an hour just wasn't enough time to give him more than an inkling of what the young men had been talking about.

"The worst of it," he told Fess, "is that none of it seems to matter much at all." Since he was alone he could speak aloud. If anyone heard him—well, all the d'Armands were strange.

That will change as you come to understand more of it, Fess assured him. *An hour a day will do wonders, Magnus.*

"I hope so," Magnus sighed. "Perhaps you can make sense of Robert's hostility, Fess. Have I violated some taboo, done something to offend him?"

No, Magnus—none.

"Then why his hostility? He almost seems to feel that I am some sort of threat to him."

Fess gave the burst of white noise that was his equivalent of a sigh and said, *Magnus, I fear I must acquaint you with some of the less pleasant aspects of Maximan heredity.*

"What?" Magnus frowned. "Adaptation to low gravity? That would effectively trap them on this asteroid. Or perhaps a chromosome for vile tempers?"

No, Magnus—inbreeding.

"Oh." Magnus's face went blank. "All of the above."

Quite right, Magnus. Recessive traits are reinforced, and some of them are desirable—but some are not. Over the centuries, some of the more un-

*pleasant traits have become widespread—such as
low intelligence and emotional instability.*

"So." Magnus thought that one over. "A surprising
number of my dear relatives will be idiots or madmen."

*Yes, Magnus, though in many cases, they will be
neither, just . . . a little slow, or rather unpleasant.*

"Which accounts for Robert." Magnus nodded.
"Nothing wrong with him but a mild case of paranoia. And what, may I ask, is the matter with Pelisse?"

Nothing that I have detected.

"Yet?"

Yet. Of course.

That also accounted for Magnus's uncle, and his
delusion. And it gave Magnus an inkling as to why
the Count's son had elected to stay on Terra. In any
event, the heir was not to be aired, and showed absolutely no interest in inheriting the family estates.

Magnus learned these details the next day, as he
was escorting Pelisse through the mall. Between
lengthy stops to chat with her friends, she managed
to answer a question or two about the family.

"It is difficult to believe that Uncle Roger has no
interest in the inheritance." Actually, Magnus didn't
find it hard to believe at all.

"I know—but he doesn't," Pelisse said, "though
it's a good guess that he'll expect a decent share of
the income."

"Of course." Magnus smiled, not pleasantly. "All

Christopher Stasheff

the money but none of the responsibility or inconvenience, eh? He won't bring it off, will he?"

"Oh, I'm sure he'll receive a generous settlement—but even if he didn't, I don't think that would persuade my dear uncle to come back." Pelisse seemed to have grown rather nervous. She stopped abruptly, facing into a store-screen. "Oh, what a lovely gown! Come, Magnus, I must try it on!"

Magnus glanced up at the gown and wondered what could have taken her eye about it; it seemed quite ordinary to him. But, all things considered, there were worse things to do with his time than to watch Pelisse try on a tight-fitting gown, so he followed her around behind the screen and into the shop, not entirely reluctantly.

38

CHAPTER
~3~

Ian waked slowly, blinking, and sat up, looking about him, puzzled. The room seemed very strange.

Then he remembered.

Nothing had changed inside the stone egg; the light was still the same. He frowned, rubbing a hand across his mouth. How could he tell what time of the day or night it was? He rose, and went slowly toward the stairway, wondering how he would get out.

There was a clicking sound behind him.

He spun about.

The voice said, "Food and drink are served."

He saw a new plate on the table with clean utensils beside it, and on the plate was a dark, thick slice of meat—a steak, and more of the wonderful bread, and something green, which must have been a vegetable. Beans? And a lump of mealy white stuff, and a tall glass filled with white liquid. He ran to the chair, suddenly aware of his hunger again. He picked up the steak in both hands, bit, and chewed. When he was done, he dropped the bone and scooped the beans into his mouth. They tasted far better than the hard, dry lentils he had always eaten, and the mealy stuff was creamy and smooth in his mouth. The white liquid proved to be cow's milk—he had drunk of it now and again—and he drank it down in huge gulps.

When he was done, he sat back, sighing. He found a square of white cloth next to the plate and wondered what it was for, then noticed the grease on his hands. Surely the cloth must be for cleaning! He picked it up and wiped off the grease; then, with another happy sigh, he got up from the table, looking about him, and feeling very, very happy.

Then he remembered that his problems had only begun. He must still get out and go to Castlerock. He could not stay in this egg for the rest of his life, delightful though the prospect seemed, for the lord to whom it belonged must come in and find him sooner or later.

He went to the stairway again. Cautiously, he climbed up, but the guardian spirit made no move to prevent him.

When he came out into the upper chamber, he went right to the wall that he had fallen through the day before—or was it only that morning? As he was raising his hand to touch it, he stopped, realizing that he had no idea how much time had passed. It might still be daylight. He frowned, and mused aloud, "How can I tell what time of day it is, when I cannot see the sun?"

A bell chimed.

Ian whirled, staring.

At the wall in front of the great chair, one of the windows had come to life. Through it, he could see the meadow outside the Great Egg, bathed in silver moonlight. He shrank back, afraid that if there were soldiers in the meadow, they might see him. Then he remembered how the dots had been there before, and came forward hesitantly, climbing up onto the chair and reaching out. He felt a hard surface beneath his fingers and realized that the guardian spirit had not really made a hole in the side of the Egg. How, then, could he see out? And if he could, surely someone else could see in! He dropped down from the chair and scurried around to hide behind it, peeking out at the "window."

It was night; he had slept most amazingly. But how was this? The guardian spirit had heard his question, and given him an answer.

Perhaps also . . .

"How may I get out from this place?" he said, aloud. He waited a moment; nothing happened. Perhaps the guardian spirit had not heard him.

Suddenly, a section of the wall over to the side of the chamber slid back. Ian stared at it in surprise, and not a little fear.

The wall was open. The night was outside. He could feel its breeze on his face.

Slowly, he picked up his staff and started toward the opening.

• • •

The music spangled and glittered in an array of high, rippling tones, while the bass notes throbbed beneath them in a rhythm that matched his pulse, then pulled it along to meld with the music's tempo. It was disconcerting, this synthesized music that was undeniably a waltz, yet far more physical than even that scandalous dance had ever been, pounding in his veins and making it seem the most natural thing in the world for his hips to gyrate, his muscles to shift against the rounded softness of Pelisse's body, so close against his, matching the beat, and with it, his movements, like a hand in a glove. He looked down at her and swallowed, his throat thick with the sensations that flooded through his body, so rare for him and yet so unpleasantly familiar.

One of the disadvantages to being so tall was that he was looking down at her upturned, shining face, and could unfortunately not help seeing the décolletage beneath it—and, though the gown was low-cut and revealing, he was sure it wasn't supposed to be so *very* revealing.

Was it?

He managed to force a smile, at least a small one, feeling his face grow hot, knowing that his eyes, at least, were filled with incredulous delight. All he could seem to see were her mouth, wide and very red, with rich, ripe lips that trembled on the verge of opening, almost begging to be caressed, tasted; the small, delightful tilt of her nose; her huge, blue eyes; and the equally huge, swelling mounds beneath her neckline. He tried to minimize the view by pressing her tightly against himself, but it was perhaps not the wisest course of action, for she murmured with pleasure, moving her hips lauguidly against his thigh, and he felt his own body responding. "Fair cousin," he whispered, his tongue thick in his mouth.

Why, then, this cool, detached part of his mind that stood back watching, and snickered?

"*Handsome* cousin," she breathed in return, eyelids lowering. "Will you not sweep me away in your ship, to some enchanted realm where only we two shall exist?"

Was that what she wanted, for him to steal her away from this gilded backwater prison? For somehow, his detached self didn't doubt that she wanted *something*.

So did he—or at least his body did. His mind, though, was apprehensive, and his heart seemed to have jelled. Did it sense something that his mind only suspected, and his body ignored?

He knew it was bad, unhealthy, to think of himself in parts in this manner, but he couldn't help it; though he ached with desire for pleasures he had never fully known, he was still reluctant, hesitant . . .

And amused.

He was shocked to realize it, and tried to banish the thought, to ignore his own cynicism, to concentrate on the desire within him, and the beautiful, provocative face turned up toward his, the sleepy eyes, the trembling lips. . . .

He brought his own lips down, to brush against hers, and felt her whole body swelling up to meet his. Then the cymbals crashed, and he pulled back, startled. They were, after all, in public.

She made a *moue* of disappointment and lowered her gaze. "Why so shy, cousin?"

"It would be a poor return for the hospitality of your family, milady," he said, "were I to seek to seduce their daughter."

She tossed her head, her laugh a ripple of brightness that the music tried vainly to echo. "Do you think they care? Such concern was for the dark ages, when intimacy meant conception. Liaisons between cousins are no shame here, Magnus, nor even cause for a frown! Especially when the two have grown up apart, and are strangers, as we are—for there can be no incest in the mind, when we are worlds apart in our origins!"

It was a pretty speech, for a culture that used the language of science as social pleasantries—and an invitation so thinly veiled that he would verge on discourtesy to refuse it.

And he was tempted, his body ached with it. . . .

Suddenly, the longing crashed through him, through his reserve; the furious desire to banish the injuries of his past by immersion in her, in her body, bathing away the aura of humiliation and heartache that had always accompanied sexual overtures in his past. Almost in a rage to banish those memories, to scourge those responses, he lowered his head again and pressed his lips to hers. They trembled beneath his, parted only slightly, only enough to entice, to invite, and he caressed them with the tip of his tongue, teasing them open, letting his mouth sink into hers, her lips warm and moist all about his, flesh sliding over flesh, awakening a thousand burning neurons to send their flame coursing throughout his body. Vaguely and distantly, he was aware that they had stopped dancing, that they stood still, engrossed in the kiss, that her whole body seemed to reach up to his in delight, in . . . triumph?

Near the wall, her cousin Robert stared, outraged, the blood suffusing his face—but the Countess Matilda smiled, and exchanged a knowing, pleased look with the Baroness.

Magnus returned to his rooms in a strange state— half euphoria, his head feeling as though it were inflated like a balloon with a vapor that held a strange and intoxicating aroma, the scent of Pelisse's perfume. But the other half was wariness, suspicion, almost a sense of foreboding. He sank down into a recliner and punched the pressure pads of the table beside it. In a second, the table delivered a tall glass of amber fluid into his hand. Magnus took a long drink, but it neither heightened the euphoria nor quenched the foreboding.

A pleasant evening, Magnus? Fess asked.

"Oh yes, very pleasant indeed! Five dances with my most attractive cousin, a long and intimate chat on the way to her room, an invitation to step in to continue the conversation, and when I declined, a very long and deep kiss! I should be ecstatic!"

But you are not? Why is that?

"That's the hell of it—I don't know!" Magnus put

the glass down too hard, but somehow it didn't break. "Pelisse is probably the most beautiful woman that I have yet had the pleasure of meeting—though with modern cosmetics, it's hard to be sure. At least, she looks to be the most beautiful. And she's sympathetic, complaisant, intimate—everything that should delight me! In fact, it does—but it also makes me nervous! Why is that, Fess?"

Could it perhaps be linked to your not accepting her invitation tonight?

Magnus nodded, short, choppy jerks of the head. "Yes—oh, most certainly yes! The instant she asked me in, I could feel all my emotional armor clanking into place! Why is that, Fess? The fruit of painful experiences I've had in the past, with willing women—all willing to be caressed, to go to bed, then to use me in any way they could? Or is there really something about Pelisse that sets my instincts for self-preservation to baring their teeth?"

Something of both, certainly, the robot mused. *As to Pelisse herself, I would be cautious with any Maximan lady—but the only element in her conduct that might give you grounds for trepidation is that she has been so quick to welcome you so very thoroughly, and has shown so very much attraction to you so very quickly.*

"Quickly! An understatement if I ever heard one! Only two weeks, and she's ready to invite me into her bed! Or at least into her room late at night—perhaps I'm just being conceited in thinking she might have made the deeper offer."

I doubt it. She certainly is showing all the signs of being willing—in entirety.

"Signs?" Something about the word focused Magnus's wariness. "What signs are you speaking of, Fess?"

Oh, letting her eyelids droop, invading your social distance, the specific sort of smile she gives you, her seeking of proximity. . .

"Yes, that's it! Just the signs, the motions! Anyone could learn them, learn how to do them! They don't have to have an ounce of sincerity behind them!" Magnus leaped to his feet and began to pace. "And that phrase you used earlier—something about 'as to Pelisse herself.' That implies that you're seeing something more than Pelisse, something that might arouse my wariness. What?"

Why . . . the situation itself, Magnus.

"The situation? What about it? New relative shows up out of nowhere unannounced, is invited to stay with the family—what should make me suspicious about that? *They* might have cause for wariness, but *me?*"

There is an uncertainty about the succession, Magnus.

"Who's going to be the next Count after my greatuncle dies?" Magnus stood still, looking up as though Fess were physically present next to him, frowning. "Why should that give me cause for wariness?"

Because it is the reason why your presence has been so unsettling to them. They thought the suc-

cession was definite, but your presence has made it once again uncertain.

"My presence? How could it? I have no interest in being Count of this bulwark against respectability!"

But they cannot know that, and would be foolish to believe you even if you said it, no matter how sincerely.

"But what claim could I possibly have?"

One every bit as good as Pelisse's. Consider, Magnus—your great-uncle is in very poor health; the family is braced for his death. His only son is determined not to return to Maxima or accept the inheritance, perhaps wisely. He has therefore abdicated in advance, since becoming Count would mean leaving Terra.

Magnus nodded, frowning. "That still does not affect me."

But the succession is patrilineal. Since the current Count has no other male offspring, the title passes to your father's elder brother—but he is mentally incompetent, and cannot inherit. His younger brother, your father, thereby became heir, but was unavailable—perhaps dead, for all his family knew; so the title would therefore pass to your Uncle Richard's daughter.

"Then I came," Magnus whispered, "and inheritance is patrilineal."

Exactly, Magnus. Your father might not be available, but you suddenly were. You are the male heir of a cadet branch, so the title and estates could legally pass to you, even though there is a female of the senior branch.

"So my claim is as good as hers!" Magnus stared. "Perhaps better! And they're all afraid that I might try to assert it! Then who knows what would happen to their standard of living!"

Be fair, Magnus. Would you wish to see a stranger come in and take a prize that you had thought would be yours?

"No, I certainly wouldn't," Magnus breathed, "and I would do everything I could to make sure I kept that prize, no matter what!"

Unfortunately true.

"An ideal resolution, isn't it?" Magnus said bitterly. "For Pelisse to marry me, thus unifying both claims! I would have the title, she would tell me what to do with it, and the family could relax! Do you think this was her own idea, Fess? Or did her mother put her up to it?"

It would be difficult to say, Magnus, but I think we might conjecture that neither lady was terribly opposed to the idea.

"But Robert was. How say you, Fess—does my cousin harbor a rather unhealthy interest in Pelisse?"

It is unhealthy only emotionally, Magnus, as they are not truly brother and sister, but were only raised as such. In fact, I have determined that they are related only in the fourth degree of consanguinity, so there would certainly be no bar to their marrying.

"Yes, and he would become Count, and have the title, the business, and Pelisse, too! Probably had the whole process well in train, in fact, until I came in and derailed it! Big muscular stranger, from outside the immediate gene pool, with the mystery of the far traveller about him—oh yes, very unfair competition for the poor fellow! No wonder he was ready to use my anatomy for fish bait! And now that I look back on this last fortnight from this perspective, I can understand the occasional glance that passed between him and Pelisse—she was enjoying his jealousy! Fess, could it be that my fair cousin returns Robert's interest?"

Perhaps, Magnus, though I certainly would not characterize such interest as a prime example of romantic love.

"No, but it's as good as she's apt to do here!"

You wrong the lady, Magnus.

"Do I? I wouldn't really characterize her interest in me as being an impassioned true love, either! More a matter of an interesting novelty, but one that would pall rather quickly—and definitely would have to be civilized and overhauled, if she were going to keep it around for any length of time! No wonder I've been wary! No wonder she's been so interested! How could I possibly have been such a blockhead!"

Certainly not a blockhead, Magnus, Fess murmured. *I would never characterize you as such, simply because you are always willing to give the other person the benefit of the doubt.*

"Yes, but I think the time has come for moderation, don't you, Fess? Time to start restricting that impulse to situations where it doesn't really matter!"

Magnus, I fear you are becoming a cynic.

"Cynic? Oh, my heavens, no, Fess! Merely a student of human nature, eh? Yes, of course. I think it's time I had a little chat with all my relatives at once. Don't you?"

Magnus, surely you would not be ungracious!

That stilled the young giant. He stood a moment in thought, then said, "Yes, I was about to be unpardonably rude, wasn't I? Not to mention being ungrateful and risking giving hurt unjustly. I'll have to be a bit more circumspect when I confront them. After all, I only wish to be helpful, don't I?"

Helpful, Magnus?

"Yes, helpful. After all, they do have a problem with the succession. It would only be proper courtesy for a guest to help them resolve it. Wouldn't it? Yes, of course."

CHAPTER
~4~

Magnus hadn't intended to risk upsetting his great-uncle, but when the Count heard that he had asked for a "family conference," the old man had insisted it be held in his bedchamber. Now Magnus sat looking about at them all, choosing his words very carefully, not wishing to hurt any of them—he should really have been feeling sorry for each one. But the feeling of outrage was still there, though firmly held down, and he couldn't completely keep his emotions out of the affair.

"Well, what is this all about then?" the old Count demanded. He stirred restlessly in his bed. "Say your piece, young man. What is it that is so important that you wish to address it to us all together?"

"Why, Uncle," Magnus said slowly, "what should it be but my thanks for your hospitality, and a farewell?"

There was instant consternation, and Magnus found it very satisfying.

"No, not so soon!"

"You mustn't, young man!"

"Come now, after all these years?

"Surely you have a duty to your family!"

Magnus rode it out, permitting himself to feel a very solid satisfaction—which was somewhat tempered by the glow of hope and delight he saw in Robert's face, and the relief in the Count and Countess.

Pelisse, though, was completely taken aback, even appalled. "So soon? And so suddenly? But Magnus, this is really too bad of you!"

"My apologies." Magnus inclined his head. "I would not have been so abrupt, or so dramatic, if recent events had not made my departure a matter of some urgency."

"Recent events?" Countess Matilda frowned. "Of what sort?"

But Pelisse had a look of foreboding for a few seconds, before she regained her composure. "Yes, Magnus. What events could you be thinking of?"

"Not events alone," Magnus said slowly, "but new information, too. I have become aware that you may be having a difficulty with the succession."

Instantly, the guards were up, the faces wore bland smiles, and the family had rushed to battle stations.

"However," Magnus said, "it really is not politic to discuss this in the presence of the current Count."

"No, no! Absolutely necessary, absolutely!" The Count waved the objection away—but anxiety shadowed his features. "How can I rest easily if there's a chance I'll leave the family in the lurch, eh? What sort of problem are you thinking of, young man? What difficulty with the succession?"

"My place in it, primarily," Magnus said slowly. "I have become aware that you all believe I may attempt to inherit, when . . . the time comes."

They should have raised a chorus of protest, they should have claimed that such a thought could not have been further from their minds—but they were silent, Pelisse wide-eyed, Robert infuriated, the Countess frightened, and the Count grave.

"The notion is ridiculous, of course," Magnus said, "or should be—but I have slowly become aware that all of you fear I may have come to Maxima for that purpose."

"Why ridiculous?" the Countess said, through tight lips.

"Why, because, on my home so far away, only the most general news of Terra and its colonies has come to us—and nothing from the family, though my father mentioned from time to time that he had attempted to send word to you. . . ."

"We received the occasional missive," the Count acknowledged, "but we had no means of replying."

Magnus reflected that they could not have tried terribly hard. "Exactly—we were isolated from you. I grew up in the assumption that Maxima was the family home, but of no other interest to me, for my father's uncle was the current Count, and his son would inherit in his turn. I never dreamed that the title might pass to the cadet branch—though I knew that if it did, my uncle would inherit, not my father. . . ."

"But you had no way of knowing that he would be *non compos mentis*." The Count scowled, nodding.

"Indeed," Magnus acknowledged. "Of course, if matters came to such a pass, it would be my father who would inherit, not I—but as you all know, he has won a title and lands of his own, and would certainly relinquish all claims to the inheritance."

"You, however, are available." Robert's eyes smoldered.

"I did not quite realize that, until yesterday," Magnus said. "It explained many things—Robert's hostility, the Countess's reticence, perhaps even Pelisse's attentions."

"You lie!" Robert leaped to his feet, face red, fists clenched.

"Really, young man!" the Countess snapped.

"Magnus!" Pelisse cried, then faltered and looked away.

Magnus held up both palms. "My apologies; I did not mean to offend. But you must understand that I grew up on the fringes of court intrigue, so it is natural to me to question every attention, even the kindnesses that Cousin Pelisse has shown me. She is truly a gentle and open-hearted woman—but a man with a suspicious mind might note that she is the current heir and that, since she is female and the succession is patrilineal, she would only inherit if there were no male to claim the title—so that my claim might be construed as being as strong as hers."

He waited for a response, but no one spoke. Eyes were wide and faces pale, but lips were sealed.

Grimly reassured, Magnus went on, "So suspicious a person might have noted that the logical way to remove the conflict was to unite the claimants—and that Pelisse might therefore have been instructed to cultivate my affections."

He expected a hot and outraged denial from the Countess and from Pelisse—but Matilda only looked away, her face pale, and Pelisse kept her gaze on the floor.

The Count glanced from one to the other with a scowl. So, then, he had not been in on it. He turned to Magnus, starting to speak—but, afraid it might be an apology, Magnus beat him to it. "Quite ridiculous, I know, and really showing only my own conceit—after all, though I would not say I was handsome, I flatter myself that being tall, muscular, and having a certain amount of presence, might make me not altogether unappealing. But, as I say, this shows only my own arrogance . . ."

"Indeed," Robert muttered.

". . . and after all," Magnus went on, "so beautiful a lady as Pelisse certainly could not be in love with me. *Could* you, Pelisse?"

"No," Pelisse admitted, though she almost strangled on the word.

Pain stabbed Magnus, even though he had already guessed the truth of it. But he kept his face grave and nodded. "No, of course not. I must ask your forgiveness, fair cousin, for having presumed to fantasize as much—but you *are* fair, after all, so I think I might be forgiven for a masculine weakness."

"Of course," Pelisse said, managing to raise a haunted gaze to him.

Robert stood silent and trembling, fists clenched, glaring hatred at Magnus.

Magnus took it as tribute and fed his confidence off the other man's dislike. "Yes, quite ridiculous, all of it—beginning with the notion that I might wish to inherit."

Instant consternation. All the minor relatives were talking at once; the Countess and Pelisse stared at him with huge, disbelieving eyes; and Robert's jaw dropped.

"Come, now!" The Count raised a hand and waited till the tumult stilled, locking gazes with Magnus. When the room was still, he said, "Not wish to inherit? Turn your back on a billion-a-year business? Wealth and power, and a title with it? How could you *not* wish to inherit?"

Angered though he was, Magnus wasn't quite vicious enough to tell the old man that he was no more interested in life imprisonment on a twenty-mile asteroid than the Count's own son had been. "Worldly considerations aside, sir, there is the matter of qualification for the position. I know little about robotics and nothing of modern industry; I haven't the slightest idea how to manage even one factory, let alone a whole complex. If I were to become Count, it would certainly be disastrous for d'Armand Automatons— and the good of the family is, after all, paramount."

He thought he had done that rather neatly.

But the Count waved these objections away. "You could learn, young man—and while you did, you would have excellent advisors. Have wealth and luxury no appeal to you?"

"No more than to any man." Magnus chose his words carefully. "But I have another title waiting for me on my homeworld, and estates and wealth with it." He didn't bother saying that Rod's title was probably not hereditary—he was sure the lands were. Never mind that he would be expected to share them with his siblings—he wasn't all that sure that he wanted to inherit on Gramarye, either. "But I wish to see something more of the universe before I tie myself down to one place. I do not yet wish to rest."

"You will, though," his great-uncle protested. "When you're tired of rambling, you will. And you'll have become addicted to the pleasures of the modern world. What of the inheritance then, eh?"

Even now too polite to say that a mere asteroid would be too small for him, Magnus assured him, "I would find a way to carve out a niche for myself, as my father has done."

"Quite sure of that, are you?" The Count looked doubtful, and he wasn't the only one.

"Quite," Magnus confirmed. "In fact, I am so sure, that I will sign any documents you wish, relinquishing my claim to the title and the company."

Everyone burst into disbelieving but delighted exclamations—except for the old Count. He kept his gaze on Magnus and rode out the hubbub. When it slackened, he raised a hand again, and gradually, the room stilled. "But what of your father?" the old man said then. "What of my nephew, eh? After all, he has the strongest claim of all. What assurance do we have that he will not show up seeking the title, eh?"

Magnus just barely managed to choke back a bark of laughter. The High Warlock of Gramarye, give up his castle and estates, his title and his world, for nothing but a tastelessly opulent mansion on an airless asteroid, where the use of the psionic powers he had discovered would have to be exercised so discreetly as to be virtually undetectable? Give up a world for *this*?

He didn't say that, of course. Gravely, he answered, "I cannot speak for my father; however, I very much doubt that Rod Gal—Rodney d'Armand will wish to give up his life's work and his world, to take over the family business. I do suspect that he will probably wish to see you again, sir, and his brother, no matter Uncle Richard's condition—but that he will not wish to stay. Assuming he can arrange transportation, that is."

"Transportation?" The Count frowned. "How could he not? He had to have a ship to get where he is in the first place, didn't he?"

Magnus felt a stab of guilt. "He did, sir, but he gave it to me, for my travels."

"You mean he's *trapped* there?" The Count shook his head, muttering—but Magnus saw the flare of hope in Matilda's eyes. "We can't have that!" the old man said. "Have to find a way to send him a ship, yes. After all, he *is* family."

"I will send an inquiry, sir," Magnus said politely, "and ask him for a formal abdication of rights to the claim—though I doubt that my father will be able to receive it"—again, the stab of guilt—"without his ship, and its guiding robot."

"But I do not wish to inherit!" Pelisse cried, then lowered her eyes instantly.

"Pelisse!" her grandmother gasped, scandalized.

Again, the Count held up a hand for silence. "What's this, Granddaughter? Not wish to inherit! But why?"

"Why, because I don't know enough," Pelisse sobbed. "I don't, Grandmother! I've studied, I've learned as much as I can, I could design and build a robot from scratch, I know all the principles of management—but I'm frightened! I can't bear the thought of having to manage the company on my own, the thought of all the members of the family who might suffer if I make too many mistakes!" She looked up at Matilda through her tears. "Can't you understand that?"

Matilda stood rigid—then, unexpectedly, thawed. She came over to her grandchild and put an arm around her shoulders. "Of course, dear, I understand—far better than you can know, in fact. But we must do what we're given to do—must do as well as we can, and hope, darling, only hope."

"You will not want for good advice," the Count muttered.

"But it is I who will have to decide!" Pelisse wailed.

"You have said yourself that you have the knowledge." Magnus frowned. "It is support you need, not advice—emotional support, the knowledge that there is someone there to depend on, if you fail."

"Of course!" Pelisse turned a tear-streaked face to him. "*Now* do you understand?"

"Quite well." Magnus held himself still against a surge of anger, then turned to nod toward his rival. "But you will pardon me for suggesting that your cousin Robert might be willing to be the staff upon which you might lean. His knowledge of these affairs is certainly far greater than mine—and, unless I quite mistake him, he would be very willing indeed."

Now it was Pelisse who froze.

Matilda lifted her gaze slowly, seeking out Robert. He braced himself visibly, and bore up under her scrutiny.

"So that is the way of it," Matilda murmured. "All the time, and right beneath my nose, too. Really, child, you might have told me."

"But you don't *approve* of Robert," Pelisse mumbled.

"As a liaison? Certainly not; he's far too wild. But as a husband? Well, when he has settled down—who can tell? I'll have to consider the matter—carefully."

The Count turned a frosty glance on his kinsman. "I think you had better be done sowing your wild oats, young man, and very quickly, too."

"Yes, sir," Robert said meekly.

"I might also suggest," said Magnus, "that your uncle the professor might find it possible, perhaps even desirable, to return to Maxima during the summers, when he is not preoccupied with teaching. What is his field?"

"Why, robotics, of course," said the Count, frowning.

Magnus restrained an urge to shout at him, and only smiled. "How perfect! Has he never asked d'Armand Automatons to test new ideas for him?"

"Well, the occasional notion . . ."

"He really should have you manufacture all his pilot models. After all, family *is* family. And I think you might find that he would be available for consultation even during his teaching terms, if his share of the family inheritance were contingent on his assistance. I was under the impression that consultancies enhanced a professor's prestige."

"What an excellent idea!" The Count stared. "Really, young man, you might find you have a gift for this sort of thing, after all."

"No, Great-uncle—only for intrigue. Which, as I've told you, permeated the very air I breathed as an infant." Magnus didn't mind the occasional exaggeration.

But Matilda frowned. "You don't know the professor as we do, young man. I doubt that he would be willing to return to Maxima even for three months at a time."

Somehow, Magnus found he could believe that.

"Must be a way." The Count scowled. "After all, family is paramount, eh?"

Magnus pursed his lips. "Perhaps I might talk to my academic cousin?"

"Well—I suppose you might, if you were willing to go to Terra."

"Has he no hyper-phone?"

"Of course—but do you really think it will do any good?"

"There is a possibility," Magnus said.

Magnus adjourned with Matilda to the communications center of the household. *Magnus*, Fess's voice said in his mind, *I hope you are not planning anything unethical.*

Is persuasion unethical? Magnus returned.

It can be ethical or unethical, depending on your methods.

Then observe my methods, and judge them when I am done, Magnus thought curtly. He didn't need his resident daemon to tell him that what he was contemplating was not completely proper. He sat with the Countess in the household's communication center. He glanced at the range of clocks above the communicator screen and noted the time in Boston, on the continent of North America. Eight o'clock in the evening—an excellent time for a family call. He glanced up at the Countess. "Will the connection be long in coming?"

"Not terribly," Matilda answered, just as the glow of the screen broke into snow, then cleared as a pastel flower blossomed from the center outwards. Words came from the flower's center, swelling to fill the screen. *You have connected with 27-14-30-260-339977AZ.*

Aunt Matilda nodded. "It is Roger's address."

Magnus frowned. "Why does he not identify himself by name?"

Matilda glanced at him with amusement and, yes,

condescension, no matter how slight. "To guard against theft." She turned back to the screen, unaware that she had left Magnus wondering how a mere display of digits could be a charm against burglary. "Please inform Professor d'Armand that his stepmother is calling."

Stepmother? Magnus concealed his surprise. Matilda was the Count's second wife, then. He wondered how that affected the succession.

The display remained constant, but the music modulated into the word, "Affirmative."

"Showy," Matilda muttered, "but cheap."

Magnus didn't understand a bit of it, so he kept his face impassive.

Then the flower faded from the screen, revealing the face of a middle-aged man, which hit Magnus with a shock. The second wife must have been a good twenty years younger than the first. He had thought it was illness that had made the Count look twenty years older than his wife, but now he realized it was simply time.

The professor had a long, pallid face, and a guarded manner. The resemblance to the Count was unmistakable. "Matilda! What a pleasant surprise!"

"And a pleasure to see you, Roger." There was real warmth under the Countess's reserve. "And let me relieve your mind before we go any further—your father is no worse, if no better."

"Glad to hear the former, and sorry to hear the latter." Roger glanced toward Magnus. "Would I be right to infer that this young man is therefore the reason for your expending so much money for this call?"

"He is my excuse," Matilda admitted. "Roger, meet your Cousin Magnus—Rodney's son."

"Rodney! Then he still lives?" The professor turned to Magnus with a quickening of interest. "We had feared that he must have fallen prey to the hazards of his profession—a secret agent's life, and all that. Is your father well, young man?"

"Yes, quite well." Magnus hid the shock of hearing his father described as a secret agent—but of course, that was what he was, though it was no longer his primary occupation. "I bring his greetings to all the family—but I must convey them to you in this fashion, since I do not expect to visit Terra." That wasn't quite true, but he was resolved to come nowhere near anyone else bearing the name "d'Armand."

"I regret to hear it." The professor frowned. "You would enjoy Cambridge—it's something of an oasis amidst the desert of the modern world."

"Is it really? I'm afraid I know so little of Terra." Even as he spoke, Magnus's mind was reaching out, following the tachyon beam inward past Mars' orbit, past Luna, seeking the mind so distant in the connection. He needed a bit more talk to have the feel of that mind, the signature, the insubstantial air that would make it distinct from all the other minds on Earth. "I gather that Cambridge is a city restricted to the pursuit of knowledge?"

"You might say that." The professor smiled. "Though so many of our research institutions are allied with commerce now, that we might more accurately say that Cambridge is devoted to the business of knowledge."

"What is the appearance of the town?"

"A strange wording; I gather that your native idiom differs from my own." The professor gave him a keen look. "Well, young man, we specialize in old buildings and new postures, if that means anything to you."

It meant more than he knew; Magnus had singled his mind out of the throng, and was letting his own consciousness filter through that of his cousin, feather-light, insubstantial, but gradually perceiving the world as the professor perceived it, soaking up his thoughts and memories. "My own world reveres the antique, Professor." That was putting it mildly— the whole culture had been modeled on an idealized view of the European Middle Ages. "It is an attitude with which I can sympathize."

"Then you must come to Cambridge and discover it for yourself." The professor smiled again, still very much on his guard. "But surely you have not taken the time to contact me simply for a description of my city, young man."

"No, but I have wished to meet you, and a discussion of the town in which you live gives me an additonal sense of your personality," Magnus answered. "I am embarked on a voyage of self-discovery, you see, and I have begun it by seeking out my roots, attempting to learn something of my father's people."

"It is a process with which every professor is familiar—he is exposed to it so constantly." Roger's features softened, his guard lowering as he gained confidence and a sense of superiority over his young caller. "What have you learned thus far?"

"That family is extremely important to all my relatives," Magnus returned, "frequently more important than their own welfare."

The professor frowned, not liking this view of the topic. "And do you find this attitude healthy?"

"It is certainly to the benefit of the family," Magnus returned, "and each individual's welfare seems to depend on that of the family. All in all, I find it conducive to the welfare of the individuals involved, yes."

"But don't you also find it somewhat restrictive?"

There was an undertone of the defensive there—Magnus pursued, and found the guilt from which it stemmed. As he talked, his mind softened the edge of that emotion, mellowing it into a feeling of obligation. "Quite restrictive, since I was born and raised on a planet not much smaller than Terra. When you have had a whole world to wander, or at least a very large island, you come to miss the outdoors."

Matilda looked up indignantly.

"I came to miss it before I had experienced it," Roger said, with a smile.

"Young men are always restless," the Countess said crisply, "and long to explore new environments. Isn't that so, Magnus?"

"I live in witness to it." Magnus allowed himself a slight smile, but his mind was sifting through the memories that the conversation brought up in Roger's mind. "I cannot help but wonder what attractions there must be on your overcrowded Terra, to make you wish to stay there."

The question brought a flood of emotions and memories, though the professor maintained a bland smile. Magnus probed delicately, following linkages of associations down to underlying attitudes. He worked very carefully; this wasn't really his gift, but he had witnessed his mother and sister doing it, and had even been on the receiving end once or twice, when he was sunk in apathy. Yes, the professor's dislike of Maxima was superficially due to a natural youthful wanderlust, but it endured for a deeper reason—what Magnus could only think of as an emotional claustrophobia, a feeling of suffocation under the presence and chatter of too many people in too small a space. Magnus examined more closely, and found memories of never-ending demands from the Countess, the Count, and a score of other relatives. Roger had been the one on whom everyone else had loaded the responsibility of recommending what to do with Uncle Richard; he had been the one who had had to support his father through the decline and death of his first wife. As one of the few really stable people in the family, he had always been the object of the others' emotional demands, had been the one who kept the rest of them functioning—and this before he was out of his teens! Magnus sympathized; in two short weeks, he had already begun to feel the attachment of those emotional tendrils, the conflicting pulls of several people at once.

Nontheless, family came first—and if Cousin

Roger wanted the financial benefits of d'Armand Automatons, he would have to shoulder some of the responsibility.

The professor was answering. "Cambridge is kept free of overcrowding, young man, except on football Saturdays. And there is a feeling of freedom, of spaciousness, that no space habitat can match."

"I concur," Magnus said. "But surely the demands of others are present in any social environment."

"Yes, but they maintain a certain degree of reserve in an academic setting," the professor began, and was off into paeans of praise for the fellowship of scholars. Beneath his words, Magnus read a dread of intimate relationships, for his familial life had been so stifling that he had not married even once, and had certainly taken pains to be sure he fathered no children. His relationships with women were fleeting, and the only intimacy was that of the body. Magnus felt a surge of empathy, recognizing a maimed soul when he saw one, and identifying with it with such intensity that it shocked him. But battle-trained reflexes took over; he pushed his own emotions to the background while he worked within his cousin's mind, inputting reassurance that the other members of the family had adjusted to his absence and had found their own sources of security without him.

Roger had finished with a description of the pleasures of sitting in the sun on an autumn morning, discussing superconductor theory with his colleagues. Magnus noted the falling inflection and murmured, "Such a web of relationships must be very pleasant, with no one pressing you for involvement."

"Yes, quite." But the professor frowned suddenly, as though a puzzle in the back of his mind had just been solved. "Rodney's son—then your claim to the succession is as valid as my cousin Pelisse's!"

"True," Magnus acknowledged, "but her claim is also as valid as mine, and she has the advantage of knowing the situation—and the greater advantage of wanting to stay on Maxima for most of her life."

"I see." Roger smiled, amused. "You are no more enamored of life on an asteroid than I, eh?" *Or of refereeing a convention of madmen,* his mind said silently.

Magnus commiserated, and made sure the older man felt the surge of emotion. "The problem is that Pelisse does not wish the authority."

"Oh, she will grow into it, by the time she has to assume the responsibility," Roger said breezily.

But Matilda contradicted him, rather severely. "That moment could come tomorrow, Roger, or even tonight."

"Or not for five years, or ten," Roger retorted, all his emotional shields up and vibrating. "Father has excellent medical care, Matilda, and you have informed me that his mind is as sharp as ever. You will pardon me if I do not show undue concern."

Matilda reddened, but Magnus said smoothly, "It is your *due* concern that is perhaps appropriate."

"Indeed." Roger turned to him angrily. "And what concern do you think is due, young man?" His tone said: *interloper.*

"That of an advisor." Magnus worked at keeping his posture loose, not letting the tension show. "After all, you have a vested interest in d'Armand Automatons, as well as an academic one, do you not?"

"Academic?" Roger frowned. "The family business is just that, young man—they apply proven principles in building their robots; they don't experiment."

Magnus looked up at Matilda in surprise that was only partly feigned. "You don't have a research and development department?"

"Well, of course," Matilda said, nettled. "They are constantly searching for new ways to apply established knowledge."

"But not to discover new principles themselves." Roger smiled vindictively. "After all, there's just so much that artificial intelligence can do, and creative thought is really beyond a cybernetic 'brain.' "

"Which means that it is for you to do the primary research," Magnus interpreted. "Surely you could see that the family has the benefit of that."

"And the rest of the world! I publish my results, young man!"

"As is only appropriate," Magnus said smoothly. "Still, you must verify your results repeatedly before you publish, must you not?"

"Yes." Roger frowned, not seeing Magnus's point.

"And if d'Armand Automatons had performed those experiments for you, they would be in a position to investigate applications much more quickly than the rest of the industry."

Roger looked off into space, mulling the thought.

"There's some point in that—but Father has never shown any interest in participating in my work." Beneath his words, Magnus caught vivid, fleeting images of loud and angry arguments, of a father's chilly silence at what he perceived as his son's abandonment and rejection.

"Have you ever asked?" Magnus said quietly.

"He has not," Matilda said, while Roger was still opening his mouth. "I confess that the idea is attractive—but such experiments would require your physical presence now and again, Roger."

Alarm flared, and Magnus was quickly calming it with the revelation that three months would never be time for entangling relationships to form again. "I assume that if d'Armand Automatons were to use your discoveries, you would expect some form of royalties."

"Of course!"

"But you receive shares in the family business already, Roger," Matilda reminded him. "Your stock in the company has never been alienated."

Roger turned frosty. "I have never used the proceeds from that stock, Matilda, not since I came to Terra and used some of the dividends to establish myself. They have sat and grown, increasing in number and value."

"Yes, I know—I do look at the books occasionally," Matilda returned tartly.

"It would seem to me," Magnus murmured, "that if you accept the family's share, you have some responsibility toward them." This time, the surge of guilt the professor felt was purely Magnus's doing.

But feel it he did, enough to frown and look more closely at Magnus. "You have some specific proposal in mind, young man."

"I do," Magnus admitted. "It is simply as I've suggested—that you spend your summers on Maxima, advising the heir on business matters and testing your new hypotheses." He was ready for the surge of alarm, of defensive distancing, and lulled it, soothed it, worked in the thought, again, that three months was too short a time to become enmeshed in a circle of endless demands.

The professor's face had turned stony, but was softening already into a thoughtful frown.

"Of course," Magnus said quietly, "during the rest of the year, you would be available for consultation by hyperadio, as you are now."

"The notion has merit," the professor said slowly. "Of course, for such services, I would expect a greater number of shares in d'Armand Automatons."

It was quite a change for a man who had virtually said he didn't really care about the money—but Magnus noted the undercurrent of emotion that confirmed his disregard for the family fortune. Above it rode the thought that, by putting matters on a business footing, he would be shielded from personal demands.

Magnus did not disabuse him of the notion; he merely said to the Countess, "That would seem appropriate."

"Quite." She was poised, but there was anticipation in her eyes. "Surely we need not wait for your father's death in order to see you again, Roger."

"Not at all, Matilda—you are perfectly free to meet me here in Cambridge at any time; you know you will be welcome," the professor assured her. "As to this summer—well, I am committed to a graduate seminar, but perhaps I could visit during the short vacation in August."

"That would be delightful," the Countess said. The slightest of smiles showed at the corners of her lips.

"I shall have to discuss it with my chairman, of course," Roger said carefully, "but there is at least the possibility."

Magnus noted that neither of them had said anything specific about how much stock the professor could look forward to receiving. It really *didn't* matter to them, after all.

And when the closing amenities had been exchanged and the professor's image had disappeared from above the black square, Matilda turned to Magnus, her face suffused with joy. "However did you manage that, young man!"

Magnus decided that she didn't really want to know.

I have observed, Magnus, Fess's voice said. *Are you certain your action was ethical?*

Resolving a family dispute, and reconciling a stepmother and stepson? Setting a man on the road to freeing himself from the fear of intimacy that has stunted his personal growth all his adult life? Certainly an ethical, deed, Fess!

About the means, though, Magnus wasn't quite so certain. He had given his cousin emotional assurances that he wasn't sure were true. Moreover, he had altered the thoughts and emotions of a man who was not an enemy, without his knoweldge or consent—and that definitely was unethical, so he did feel rather guilty. Not too much so, though—he had adjusted a neurosis, and had left the man better than he had found him. Besides, he could always plead necessity.

Then too, Roger *had* been evading his responsibility—and family *was* family.

"It was amazing!" Countess Matilda was flushed with excitement, sitting by the Count's bed and talking to the whole family. "Nephew Magnus spoke very quietly and reasonably, even sympathetically—and Roger saw his point at once!"

Pelisse stared. "You mean he didn't lose his temper?"

The Countess colored. "No, and I did not even have to speak sharply with him! Really, your Cousin Magnus is most persuasive!"

"It is primarily a matter of seeing an equitable solution that is beneficial to all parties." Magnus felt rather uncomfortable under such effusive praise, especially since he knew just how he had done what he had done. "And, of course, such a solution is more easily seen by one who is external to the situation."

"But I hope you will not feel that you are outside the family!" Pelisse turned a beaming face upon him—and Magnus felt a surge of the selfsame alarm he had felt in Cousin Roger. The tendrils of demand were already reaching out for him, with no compensating benefits. "I will, of course, delight in my name, and my background," he lied. "I am honored to have helped in resolving your problems with the succession—and to know that you can manage quite well without me."

A look of triumph lit Robert's face, but Pelisse was startled, and the Countess was suddenly pensive. "Surely you do not intend to leave us so soon, young man!"

"I fear I must." Magnus inclined his head politely. "I have limited time to learn of my background, and have many more courses to run. For example, I believe I will accept Cousin Roger's invitation, so that I may see something of Terra, the source of us all."

"Laudable." The Countess couldn't really object, if he was visiting family—and reinforcing the miracle he had just worked on Roger. "Surely you will visit us soon after, though?"

"I look forward to the event," Magnus assured her. Indeed, he could look forward to it so well that he didn't intend to let it happen. "Since I must depart today, I am glad to have been of some slight service to you."

"Today!" Pelisse cried; and,

"No, really!" the Countess said.

But the Count nodded gravely, and only said, "You must allow us to express our gratitude in some way, young man."

"I have scarcely made a fitting return to your hospitality," Magnus objected.

A trace of guilt flitted across Matilda's face, and

Pelisse lowered her eyes; they were shamed, for they knew just how insincere their hospitality had been.

So did the Count. "You must, at least, have some token from the family, some talisman that will remind you of your roots, and of our gratitude!" He turned to his wife. "My dear, see that the young man is given one of our latest TLC robots, with a selection of bodies and a yacht to house them."

Matilda nodded, but Magnus stared in alarm, feeling the shadow of obligation. "Surely that is far too generous, Uncle!"

"You underestimate the service you have done us," the Count said, but Magnus could not help feeling the emotion that fairly blasted from the man— his shame and embarrassment, for he knew very well how they had sought to exploit their guest.

Magnus realized that if he did not accept the gift, they would find ways to keep after him, insisting on expiating their guilt—but if he accepted this token, they would be able to relax and forget him.

"Besides," the Count said, "you have told us that you have old Fess and your father's ship, which leaves him devoid of transportation, should he wish to visit us—and even devoid of communication! No, no, we must be able to congratulate him on his hardwon rank, and to thank him for your visit! You really must accept a robot of your own, Nephew!"

Magnus stilled. It was an alluring prospect, having a robot that had not served five hundred years of his ancestors before him—having a companion that he had won himself, no matter how badly overpaid he might be.

And after all, what else did the d'Armands have to offer that was really of them?

Magnus, Fess's voice said, *your father has given me to you, and made you my owner.*

But there is merit in what he says, Magnus thought back, *and I would feel forever guilty if I deprived Father of you for the rest of his life—especially when an alternative is available.*

He was rather hurt that Fess didn't try to argue him out of it.

CHAPTER
~5~

Ian stepped through, and the panel hissed behind him. He turned, to find only the blank stony surface of the Egg, pitted and rain-washed. He could see no seam. It looked for all the world like a great gray stone again. He turned away, shaking his head and marveling.

Then he remembered that he was out in the open once more, and that the keeper, or even soldiers, might still be looking for him.

He ran quickly and lightly to the cover of the nearby woods, trying to move as quietly as he could. He threaded his way between the trees, looking for a path. He found none, but finally saw a glint in the night and heard the warbling of water swirling. He pushed through the underbrush and found a small stream, sparkling in the moonlight and babbling to itself like an idiot. He was thirsty; he dropped his staff, went down on his hands and knees, and drank.

As he lifted his head, he saw a man sitting across the stream from him.

Magnus stared up through the port beside the airlock, amazed at the size of the ship. "All this, for only one man?"

"Two, if necessary," Matilda answered, "and for a year or more. It is a home away from home, and has to store food and water for twelve Terran months, as well as a selection of robot bodies for the 'brain,' and everything our experts can think of, for survival on a strange planet."

Magnus was awed. This close to the ship, it seemed vast, a great golden disk whose rim was twenty feet in the air. Beside it, the converted asteroid that was his father's ship seemed small and inconsequential.

Then Magnus noticed the cable connecting the two ships. He frowned and was about to ask, but even as he opened his mouth, the cable disconnected from Fess's ship and reeled slowly back into the golden disc, waving like a snake charmer's cobra in the negligible gravity. "Why were the two ships connected?"

Aunt Matilda looked blank. "Why, I've no idea."

Magnus shrugged it off; the matter seemed inconsequential. He gazed up at the huge ship, sitting in golden splendor amid the desolation of the airless asteroid, and felt exalted at the mere thought that it was *his* ship, now. "It is magnificent!"

"Not quite as noble as it looks," Aunt Matilda said, amused. "The color is due to a superconducting finish that allows the most effective force-field ever developed, to be erected around the ship with far less energy than ever before."

"I am glad it has a utilitarian excuse," Magnus answered, "for I will feel sinfully sybaritic in such a craft. What did my uncle term it—a TLC?"

"That is its model number," Aunt Matilda explained. "It stands for 'Total Life Conserver,' since it is equipped to protect the lives of its passengers in every way known, up to and including cryogenic freezing, if all else fails."

"Reassuring," Magnus murmured.

"It has a serial number, of course," Matilda went on, "but it also has a more personal designation, connoting its strength and abilities—Hercules Alfheimer."

"Hercules Alfheimer?" Magnus stared. Hercules, of course, was the great hero of the Greeks—but Alfheim was the home of the light elves of the Norse. "You don't mind mixing your mythologies, do you?"

The Countess's eyes glowed, and Magnus suddenly realized that he'd apparently passed some sort of unexpected test. "Quite so, Nephew," she said. "We try to do that with every new robot, to indicate that it is not restricted to the world-view of any one culture. Naming gives it a more convenient designation than its serial number alone, and one which helps to humanize its behavior."

Both of which made it seem less intimidating to the humans who had to deal with it, Magnus realized.

"When it is sold, of course," Matilda went on, "its new owner can change its name to whatever he or she pleases."

Magnus intended to; the collision of cultures jarred on his sensibilities. "I will treasure it, Aunt. I thank you deeply."

"Think of us always," she admonished. "Now, if you must leave, young man, you must. Do come again."

"It shall be a matter of great anticipation," Magnus assured her. "My thanks to you, Aunt Matilda, and to my uncle . . ." He turned to Pelisse and therefore necessarily toward Robert, who stood behind Pelisse with his hand touching her shoulder, still defiant as he stared at Magnus—but forcing a smile now, at least. "Farewell, cousins," Magnus said. "My life is richer for knowing you."

"Oh, not farewell!" Pelisse was dewy around the lashes. "Say only, 'till we meet again!' "

"*Au revoir*, then," Magnus said, trying to make his smile warm. "This has been an unforgettable experience." He reached out to squeeze her hand, then turned away and made his escape into the boarding tunnel.

He came out into the ship; the hatch dogged itself behind him, and a soft, deep voice said, "Greetings, Master Magnus."

"I am pleased to make your acquaintance, Hercules Alfheimer." Magnus inclined his head, remembering what his father had told him: *Be polite to robots, even if they don't need it—it'll keep you in the habit of being polite to people.* Magnus already knew how thoroughly all human beings are creatures of habit.

"Thank you, Master Magnus," the robot's voice answered.

" 'Magnus' alone will do," the young man said. "I have no wish to have one call me 'master'; adjust it in your programming."

"Noted," the computer replied. "My name, too, can be changed to suit you, Magnus. I have found that most human beings prefer to shorten long designations."

"Indeed." Magnus nodded. "Let us make a contraction of 'Hercules Alfheimer': 'Herkimer.' " He smiled; there was something amusing about so grand a ship having so modest a name.

" 'Herkimer' I shall be henceforth," the computer agreed. "Would you like a tour of the ship, Magnus?"

"After we are in space," Magnus said. "For now, I would like to be away as quickly as possible."

"The control room is straight ahead," Herkimer informed him.

Magnus nodded; he had surmised as much, from the blunt ending of the corridor inside the airlock. He paced forward a dozen steps and found himself looking through an open doorway into the bridge. To his right was a drop shaft; to his left . . . "What is this hatch across from the elevator?"

"A bunkroom, for those occasions when you wish to sleep near the bridge," Herkimer answered. "There is a more fitting bedchamber below."

Magnus could just bet there was. Judging from his

guest quarters in Castle d'Armand, it was going to be such a swamp of luxury that he'd probably prefer the bunkroom permanently. He nodded, stepped through the door, sat down on the control couch—and suddenly felt that the ship was really his. "Warm your engines and plot a course for . . ." Magnus paused; he hadn't thought this far ahead. Then he shrugged; he wanted to get to Terra sooner or later. "Plot a course inward, toward the sun; we will adjust it in space."

"Very good, Magnus."

Magnus was barely aware of the most subtle of vibrations; somewhere in the ship, machinery had come to life.

One final matter remained. "A communication channel to Fess, please."

"Here, Magnus."

That had been suspiciously fast. "Fess, you are once again the property of Rod Gallowglass, *nee* Rodney d'Armand, High Warlock of Gramarye. You are to return to him as quickly as possible."

"Understood, my former master. You will understand, though, Magnus, that I leave you with some trepidation."

"You may take it with you; I already have enough trepidation to last me a lifetime."

"A feeble attempt at humor, Magnus."

"Perhaps, Fess, but I have become wary of sentiment. I will treasure your regard; and you may be as sure as any may, of my safety."

"That is my cause for concern, Magnus."

Magnus smiled. "Still, we must bear it, old com-

panion. Farewell, till I see you again on Gramarye!
Give my love to my parents and Cordelia, and my
warmest regards to my brothers."

"I shall, Magnus."

"Depart for Gramarye now, Fess. May your trip be
smooth."

"And yours, Magnus. Bon voyage!"

A surge of feeling hit Magnus, and he might have
said more, but Herkimer's voice murmured, "Ready
for liftoff."

"Which shall lift off, Maxima or we? Neverthe-
less, let us go."

There was absolutely no sense of motion—after
all, it didn't take much acceleration to escape from
so small a worldlet. But escape they did, and Magnus
felt a massive surge of relief. "Viewscreen on,
please."

The screenful of stars before him faded into a view
of the "castle," with the boarding tunnel curving out
of the eastern wing. The rough, pitted form of Fess's
ship stood by it, dull in the merciless sunlight. As
Magnus watched, the lumpy ball rose and drifted upward, but away from them, toward the constellation
of Cassiopeia. When it was well away from the surface, it began to accelerate, dwindling rapidly. Magnus watched as his last contact with home
diminished, feeling suddenly very much alone. Just
before the ship shrank from sight, Magnus murmured, "Farewell, companion of my youth. You
shall ever be with me."

"You may be sure of that, Magnus," Fess answered. "Farewell."

Then he was gone, and Magnus was staring at the screen, not at all sure he liked that last remark. "Herkimer—what did he mean?"

"There was insufficient information in his last remark, Magnus; I would have to conjecture almost blindly."

But Magnus was developing a nasty conjecture of his own. "Why were the two of you connected by cable, just before I came aboard?"

"Why, for a data transfer, Magnus."

"Indeed." Magnus braced himself. "What data was transferred?"

"The entire contents of his memory, Magnus, except for personal matters that his previous owners wished kept confidential."

Magnus's heart sank. "You now know all that Fess knew?"

"Everything, Magnus, with the exceptions noted previously."

"Including my entire biography."

"As much of it as Fess knew, yes."

Fess had been right—he would always be with Magnus. "Well, it is good to have reminders of home," Magnus sighed. "But, Herkimer?"

"Yes, Magnus?"

"You do understand that it is not necessary to tell everything you know?"

"Of course, Magnus. Any personal information of yours shall not be disclosed to anyone but you."

"That, of course," Magnus said, "but I was more concerned with family history. You understand that there is no reason to seek to impress me with the importance of the d'Armands, or the obligations of my rank?"

"Why ever should I wish to do that?" Herkimer said, in tones of mystification.

"I can't think of a single reason—but Fess could, and did." Magnus breathed a sigh of relief.

Then he breathed another, realizing that he was finally, really away from that cloying and clinging excuse for a Maximan family. It came to him that he had narrowly escaped the exact mesh of entangling relationships his cousin Roger had feared. Magnus found himself wondering if perhaps he had not betrayed the man, then wondered if he had not himself shirked his responsibilities. "I know that I must be my brother's keeper," he muttered, "but must I also watch over my cousins?"

"They are not your burden, Magnus," Herkimer replied.

Magnus looked up, startled, then realized that he had phrased it as a question. He was oddly reassured by the machine's response. It might be logical, but it lacked humane considerations, and was therefore not necessarily ethical—but it was still reassuring.

Which brought another matter to mind. "Herkimer—if you have all Fess's data, you are aware of my . . . talents?"

"Your psionic abilities?" Herkimer asked. "Yes, Magnus, I am—and I know those of your brothers and sister, and your mother and father, as well."

"And my grandfather, no doubt, and all of the rest of the knowledge of Gramarye." Magnus relaxed another stage; he could talk freely about home, if he wanted to. "Then you will understand that I have been raised with certain ethical standards in regard to the use of those abilities."

"I am so aware, yes."

"And you are aware that I used them to influence my cousin Roger?"

"That was included in Fess's briefing."

"And that such use violated my ethical code?"

The robot was silent for a half-second, then said, "I cannot truly discriminate, Magnus. There were extenuating circumstances."

But Magnus knew, and knew well. To get himself out of a bind with his relatives, he had violated a major ethical principle: he had altered the memories and emotions of a human being who was not an enemy, and without that person's permission. In retrospect, he thought he might perhaps have committed the equally unethical, but lesser, offense, of just walking out on his relatives with words of rebuke.

Though truly, he could see no third choice. There might have been one, and he could have stayed till he had found it—but that would have taken months, perhaps years, and by the time he'd been able to see it, he would have become too deeply enmeshed in the family's troubles to be able to free himself.

But that still did not excuse the violation he had committed. He had allowed his integrity to be breached, and his corruption had begun.

He wondered how much further it would go before he would be able to halt it.

Especially since he found that he had no wish to. Now that he was clear of Maxima, he could let his guard down, let himself go, let himself feel the hurt and the pain—and the anger at Pelisse and her grand-mother surged white-hot through him. How dare they toy with him, how dare they seek to use him so, to exploit him! Hadn't they realized that they would degrade him thereby? And themselves?

The whole matter left a very bad taste in his mouth, and great bitterness in his heart. He felt a sudden craving to wash out the one and assuage the other. "Herkimer! Set course for Ceres City!"

"As you wish, Magnus," the computer replied—then, almost in an echo of Fess, "Are you sure?"

"Quite sure," Magnus snapped. Ceres City—which, Fess had taught him, was a sink of iniquity, to be well avoided by any young man not wishing to be dragged down into degradation. His father had been much more succinct. "Ceres City is Sin City," he had said. "If you ever get to the Solar System, stay away from it, unless you really want to be tempted."

Magnus was in a mood to give in to any tempta-tion that came to hand. If he was going to be cor-rupted, he wanted to get it over and done with.

"Seal the hatch when I've stepped through it," Magnus told Herkimer, "and don't open it for anyone but me."

"Confirmed," Herkimer answered. Then some data from Fess's memory banks must have nudged him, because he said, "I hope you won't do anything rash, Magnus."

"Never fear," Magnus assured him. "Everything I do will be well thought out." And he stepped through the hatch, intent on a very well-considered and thoroughly planned drunk.

He paced through the boarding tunnel and out into the concourse. He looked about him, dazed by the dazzle and glitter of advertising messages and direction signs. A circle of gambling machines filled the rotunda, and asteroid miners and merchant crews and passengers came pounding off their ships to start feeding credit cards into the slots of the mechanical bandits. A 30-degree arc of the rotunda wall was taken up by a mammoth bar, and young and shapely men and women strolled around the edges of the crowd in tight-fitting body suits of dark colors. As Magnus watched, one young woman's suit suddenly turned transparent around her right breast. She glanced down at it, then up toward a man who was staring at her. The body suit turned opaque again, but another circle turned transparent, highlighting a different portion of her anatomy. Smiling, she strolled toward her prospective customer, hips rolling. Magnus glanced about and saw that the others who were similarly clad were developing transparent circles that came and went in response to the stares of the passers-by. If it was like this in the spaceport area, what would it be like in the corridors of the city proper?

Magnus felt his hormones stir at the display of dancing circles, and turned away just in time to avoid a young woman who was homing in on him. Feeling slightly sick, he stepped over to the bar, ordered a shot of straight grain whiskey, paid for it with one of the coins his cousins had given him, drank it straight down, and turned to follow the signs that promised a way out.

"Hey, fella, what'cha lookin' up?"

Magnus turned, surprised. Could someone really be talking to him?

It was a slender youth with shortish hair and very old eyes, fine-boned features, and a sinuous walk inside a body suit which was, fortuitously, totally opaque. "Saw y' walk away from the skirt, pard. Interested in a little something else?"

It came to Magnus that he was being propositioned. He felt that odd sort of locking within him, and his face went neutral. "I thank you, no. My plans for the evening are already fixed."

"Tightwad," the young man said contemptuously. His left hip went suddenly transparent. He glanced at it, then up on a line with it, and saw a matronly looking, lumpy woman with hot eyes. Instantly forgetting Magnus, he strolled toward her.

The sickness settled by the whiskey rose again, and Magnus followed the signs down the concourse and through the automatic iris that passed for a door.

The corridor was ten times what the concourse had been, except that the businesses themselves were hidden by partitions with doors. Floating glare-signs and moving, three-dimensional displays lined the sides of the broad thoroughfare, making very clear what sort of goods or services were purveyed behind each door. In the center, overhead, dancing displays advertised various brands of products. Magnus was overwhelmed by simple profusion—and by the decadence of it all. Suddenly, he was glad that he had begun his introduction to modern civilization with the much smaller-scale milieu of Maxima. He had studied all of this in Fess's data banks and 3DT displays, and it had prepared him for this, but not enough—the physical reality of it was stupefying.

So he cut it down to size. He took the first display that showed liquor pouring from an antique bottle into a glass, and went through the door.

There was a bar against one wall, tables and chairs in the center, and a line of closed booths against the far wall. Magnus could only imagine what went on in such privacy, and from the moans and gasps, he wasn't sure he wanted to know. Looking at the displays behind the bar, he realized why—there were at least as many drugs on display as there were liquors.

"Name your poison," said the man with the smoking dope-stick and traditional sleeve-garters, and Magnus didn't doubt that he meant it. He scanned the bottles and pointed to something in a fluorescent purple. "That one."

"Aldebaran Bouncer?" The man shrugged. "Your life, citizen." He punched a combination on the machine in front of him. "Thumbprint."

A glowing square appeared in front of Magnus, and he rolled the ball of his thumb across it. Didn't they need to see the card?

Apparently not; the bartender nodded, satisfied, and took a brimming glass from the machine. He set it in front of Magnus.

Magnus stared; he hadn't known it would be so large.

"'Smatter? Don't like it?"

Magnus shrugged, hoisted the tumbler, and drank. It seared his throat, and he could feel the fire trail all the way down into his belly, but it felt good somehow, burning away the shame that had soiled him within. He set the glass down, inhaled long and hard, and found the bartender staring at him. Magnus caught his breath, nodded, and said, "Good. Another."

The bartender shook himself, shrugged, and said, "Your funeral. Thumb it again."

Magnus rolled his thumb, and the bartender set another livid purple glass in front of him. Magnus took a bit longer with this one—it must have lasted two minutes. As he lowered the empty, he looked up to see the bartender watching him with a speculative look. "A girl?"

"Several of them." Magnus pushed the empty glass toward him.

"Several!" The bartender snorted. "Lucky bozo! I'm doing good to get turned down by one! Thumb it."

Magnus rolled his thumb across the plate and settled down to a single swallow at a time. He was beginning to feel numb inside, and that was good, very good. He studied the people around him, and found that a disconcerting number of them seemed to be looking his way. He scowled and locked stares with them, straightening to his full height, and one by one, they found something more interesting to look at—

Except for one man—in his thirties, at a guess—who was nowhere as tall as Magnus but had arms far longer than they should have been, and shoulders to match. He grinned back into Magnus's glare and shuffled over toward him.

"Hey now, Orange!" the bartender snapped. "Let the kid alone!"

"Alone?" Orange stepped up close, grinning up at Magnus. "I wouldn't think of it. You peaceable, kid?"

Magnus recognized a push for a fight when he saw one. Joy lit within him—at least it was something clean! " 'Orange'?" he said. "What sort of name is that?"

"Short for 'orangutang.' Wanna make something of it?"

"Juice," Magnus said.

"Not in here!" the bartender yelped.

Orange grinned around at the crowd. "You're all my witnesses—he tried to put the squeeze on me." He lifted his hands, balling them into fists.

The bartender lifted *his* hand—with a nasty-looking little blaster in it. "O*ut*!"

"Why, how inhospitable," Magnus murmured. "But I was never one to stay where I wasn't wanted." He turned away to the door. Behind him, Orange grunted, "Then how come you're still on Ceres?"

"You don't want me, then?" Magnus said as he stepped through the door and pivoted about.

"Just for a target," Orange snapped, as his fist slammed into Magnus's midriff.

Magnus rolled back, not quite fast enough; the punch hurt, and for a few seconds, his breath was blocked. But he caught Orange's fist, sidestepped, and yanked, and sent the shorter man sprawling into the wall of spectators, of whom there seemed to be an increasing number—and two of them were moving from person to person, punching the keys of their noteboards. Several of the bystanders obligingly shoved Orange back on his feet, and he snarled, leaping in and out, feinting, then slamming a quick combination of punches at Magnus's belly and jaw. The second shot at the face clipped Magnus on the cheek; he recoiled and ducked around and in, under Orange's next punch, and up, hauling him by his shirt-front and throwing him. But one of those long arms snaked out and snagged itself on Magnus's neck, throwing him off-balance and pulling him down. Magnus stumbled into a fist, staggered back as two more hit him, then caught the third and threw Orange away, shaking his head to clear it and seeing two copies of the human gorilla as he stepped back in, hand grabbing at a flat pocket against his hip . . .

. . . and coming out with a knife that flicked open, its blade glowing.

Magnus stepped back, recognizing a force-blade from its descriptions. The cleanliness of punch and pain was suddenly soiled, but not much, for he parried the arm with the blade twice, then caught the wrist with his right hand and slammed an elbow back into Orange's solar plexus. The shorter man doubled over, gagging; Magnus twisted the blade out of his grip and backhanded him on the side of the head. Orange stumbled into the cheering spectators—there were three times as many of them now, and four men with noteboards moving among them.

The nearest watchers obligingly shoved Orange out again. He was game, he swung at Magnus even now, but the young giant blocked the clumsy punch easily and slammed a right to his jaw. Orange folded and slumped to the ground.

Magnus stood, staring down at the man, teeth bared in a grin, heaving deep breaths. He reached down and hauled Orange to his feet with a surge of fellow-feeling. "Good fighting, friend. I'll stand you to the next drink."

"If he can stand to drink," someone said, but Orange only snarled and shoved Magnus away, then tottered back toward the bar. Magnus was about to go after him when he realized he was hearing a high, shrill sound, and the men with the noteboards stopped their collecting and paying-off to call, "Peace-ers!"

The crowd melted on the instant, leaving Magnus standing alone, looking about him, startled.

"Time to disappear, friend," said one of the men as he passed, stuffing his noteboard into one pocket and currency into another.

Magnus took his advice and hurried away. Glancing back, he saw an armed and uniformed man with a pack on his back, floating through the air and descending toward the bar where Magnus had just been.

Another man with a noteboard passed in the other direction, punching numbers and advising, "Stay out in the open, and the bystanders will point you out to the Peace-er. Better find another bar, pal."

Magnus did. He found three more. And three more

fights. He was drawing larger and larger crowds, and more and more of the little men with the note-boards—until the last fight turned into a full-fledged brawl. That was when he found the Peace-ers. Or they found him.

He didn't remember it, though. He only remembered ducking, but not fast enough, and the fist exploding in his face.

Then he was coming to, his head and chest one huge ache. He tried to sit up, which was a definite mistake, because his stomach suddenly convulsed, and everything he had downed the night before started back up.

Someone shoved a bucket under his face and growled, "In here, slob. I'm not cleaning up after you."

Magnus was horrendously sick for what seemed an inordinately long time. When his stomach finally stopped contracting, he managed to straighten up and lean back against something very hard, fumbling out a handkerchief and wiping his face, feeling much better inside but very, very shaky.

"Improved," someone said critically, and Magnus looked up to see a uniform with a face at the top. Over the breast pocket were the letters "E.D.G.A.R."

"Go 'way, Edgar," he groaned. "Come back for m' funeral."

"That's not the way you check out of here, pal," the guard said, "and the name's not 'Edgar.' "

Magnus frowned, trying to make sense out of that. "Says so on y'r pocket."

The guard's face came closer, frowning. "Boy, you *are* from out of town, aren't you? E.D.G.A.R. stands for the Eleusinian Drinking and Gambling Addiction Reformatory."

"Eleusinian?" Then Magnus remembered—in Classical Greece, the cult of Ceres centered around the Eleusinian Mysteries. He wished he hadn't thought of it—the effort made his headache worse. He aimed himself at the bunk and fell, groaning, "Jus' wanna die."

But the guard caught him and turned him around so that he sat instead of lying down. "'Fraid not just now, pal. You've got a visitor. Here, drink this." A rough hand hauled his head back and shoved a cup at him. Magnus opened his mouth to protest, but fluid gushed over his tongue, and he had to swallow or choke, then swallow again, and again. When the flow stopped, he pushed the cup away with a grimace. "Iyuch! What was that stuff?"

"H & I."

Magnus peered up at the man's face, squinting his eyes against the light. "What? H and I?"

"Gemini Hangover and Intoxication Oil, from Castor Epsilon. You had yourself a real time last night, spacer."

"I'm not—" Magnus cut the words off—he *was* a spacer now! The realization gave him an odd feeling, perhaps even an exhilarating one—but his body felt so horrible, he would never have noticed. "Analgesic?"

"You just had one," the guard informed him. "It'll take effect in a few minutes, but time's the only thing that's going to wipe out the aches from the punches you took. On your feet, spacer—you've got company."

"Company?" Magnus looked up, frowning, then clamped his jaw against the urge to cry out as the guard yanked him to his feet. He almost slumped onto the man's shoulder, but managed to catch hold of the bars and hold himself upright.

Bars?

Magnus finally looked up at his surroundings—bare plasticrete walls, uncovered toilet, sink, and freshener. "I'm in prison!"

"Jail," the guard told him. "Just the drunk tank—for prison, you get a trial first. Not that you won't, if anybody gets serious about those brawls last night. Let's go see your guest, now."

Magnus stared. "I'm a stranger! Who'd want to talk to me?"

"About a dozen lawyers, considering how many brawls you wound up in, and how much furniture and glassware got wiped out. Don't worry, though—the bookies will probably put up your bail."

Magnus let the man lead him out of the cell, befuddled. "Bookies?"

"You *are* green, aren't you? Every time you got in a fight last night, the bookies laid out odds and took bets. As the night went on, they had to give higher and higher odds in your favor, but they started betting on you themselves. Oh, they made a pile off of you, all right, up until the last fight—and even then, they won, because you downed the guy who started the fight with you, before his friends piled in and swamped you. Not that you were alone—everybody who laid their bets on you piled in on your side. It was one hell of a brawl, from what I hear," he said reverently. "Wish I'd been there."

Magnus decided that the people of Ceres City were very, very strange. So was the Castor oil—it was taking effect, and the pain of his bruises was dulled, the pounding in his head almost gone. "Who is this who wishes to speak with me?"

"Dunno," said the guard, "but she's one hell of a looker. If that's what they sent every time you got drunk and disorderly, there wouldn't be a man in Ceres City who wasn't in jail." He opened a plain metal door. "In you go, spacer. You sit in your chair, she sits in hers. Don't try to go over to her, or you'll trigger the alarm in the force-screen. Good luck."

Magnus stumbled into the blank, featureless room, started to turn back toward the guard with a protest on his lips—then out of the corner of his eye, saw the woman who was waiting for him, and the protest died aborning. He turned slowly, staring— she was easily the most beautiful creature he had ever seen, save one. Of course, he had been saying that about every woman who had caught his fancy in the last few months—but it had always been true. How unfair of the women, to keep becoming more and more beautiful! How was a man to hold himself back from them?

But even at the thought, he could feel the shield closing about his heart. It still ached at the loveliness of long blonde hair, retroussé nose, huge dark eyes, and full red lips—but he could contain himself; his heart stayed in his chest, not on his sleeve, and he was able to hide his feelings behind an imperturbable mask. He bowed slightly. "Good day, madame—or mademoiselle."

"Mademoiselle." She smiled, amused, and her voice was a husky breath of sensual speculation. "You're very formal, spacer."

"Until I have been introduced, or we come to know each other well." Magnus's knees were trying to turn to jelly—hopefully only from the aftereffects of his night on the town. "May I sit?"

"Of course." The woman waved to the chair facing her, surprised. "You certainly *are* rigidly formal!"

Magnus frowned as he sat; he didn't consider good manners a matter of rigidity—but, then, he had grown up with them. "To what do I owe the pleasure of this visit?" He regretted the word "pleasure" as soon as it was out of his mouth, and rightly—the woman caught it and smiled lazily, her eyelids drooping. "I hope it will lead to . . . pleasure . . . for both of us—even though I don't know how to address you. What is your name?"

Magnus opened his mouth, but caution made him hold back his real name. He substituted the first one that came to mind. "Ed . . ." he started, then realized it was the initials over the guard's pocket he was giving. But it was too late to change now, so he finished, " . . . gar."

"Ed Gar." The woman nodded, but didn't write it down. Frowning, Magnus looked more closely at her.

The brooch she was wearing ostensibly served no purpose other than decoration; but he was willing to bet it was a recording device. She said, "I am Allouene. You carry no identification."

"I left it aboard ship," Magnus told her. "I did not wish to chance losing it."

She smiled as though she did not believe him, then let the smile soften into a lazy, sensuous sultriness as she looked him over more closely. When she lifted her gaze back to his eyes, the sultriness had become an invitation, though not a burning one.

It came to Magnus, with a surge of outrage, that the woman knew exactly what she was doing, knew each intonation and lilt and shade of expression and what its effect would be on him, and was turning them on and off as though they were the keys of an organ—but it wasn't an organ she was playing, it was him.

The anger was good—it annealed the seal around his heart, strengthened his guard against her. "I am not aware of having met you previously, mademoiselle—to my regret."

The laziness focused with amusement. "You haven't. I'm only an interested bystander—or I was last night. I saw you fight Orange at the Shot and Bottle, and I was impressed with your style."

Style? Magnus had been deliberately trying for clumsiness, to make the fight last! "I was scarcely at my best."

"So I noticed. I joined the crowd that followed you from bar to bar. The drinks only affected your temper, not your reflexes. Your style improved with the quality of your antagonists."

"My antagonists improved?"

"Oh, yes." Allouene smiled, moistening her lips and shifting in her chair. "Word spread along the street, you see, and all the toughs with reputations came out to try you. They had to wait in line, I'm afraid, and they finally grew impatient and all piled in at once at the end."

"I don't really remember much of it," Magnus confessed.

"Of course not; the last bartender handed you a loaded drink to get you out of his place. I watched it all closely, though."

Magnus tried to hide his disgust. "You must be quite the aficionado of martial arts."

"Not at all," she said. "I'm a representative for a secret agency—quite legitimate, I assure you—and your display, and the emotions that seemed to accompany it, made me think you might be just what my employers are looking for."

Magnus stared, amazed.

"If you are interested in joining us," Allouene said, "we'll take care of any damages you owe, and whisk you out of this jail and off to one of our training centers." Her tone dropped to load the offer with double meaning: "Are you interested?"

His hormones thrilled, but so did the wariness of alarm. Magnus held himself immobile and asked, "What is the name of your agency?"

"The Society for the Conversion of Etraterrestrial Nascent Totalitarianisms," she answered.

Magnus stared at her, frozen with shock. She had named his father's organization! Had they followed him here from Gramarye? Had the time-travel organization that worked with SCENT alerted them to his presence here?

But no, she had asked his name, had said he was unidentified. Suddenly, Magnus was very glad he had given a false name, had left his identification aboard his ship. She was interested in him for himself alone—or at least, for his ability as a fighter.

If she was telling the truth.

"You seem shocked," Allouene said. "I assure you, we're not a bunch of bloodthirsty sadists. We're rather idealistic—our mission is to help backward planets develop the institutions that will enable them to eventually evolve some form of democratic government, and make it last. We have a strict code of ethics, and we work hard at maintaining it."

Magnus nodded. "I have . . . heard of you."

"We are a legitimate department of the Decentralized Democratic Tribunal," Allouene went on, "and if the government of the Terran Sphere isn't enough of a recommendation, I don't know what is."

Magnus had plenty of recommendations of his own to bring. He had known SCENT from birth, at least by what his father and Fess had told him of it, and had secretly treasured the notion of someday joining them himself, and going forth to free the oppressed. But as he'd grown older, he'd begun to be concerned about living in his father's shadow.

Now, however, he was being recruited in his own right—perhaps. "Is SCENT so hard-pressed for agents that you must recruit every brawler you find?"

"Certainly not," Allouene said, with a contemptuous smile. "You're a rather exceptional brawler, you know, and not just because of your size. You show a great deal of skill—and there's an intensity about you that speaks of the disillusioned idealist."

Magnus sat rigid, amazed. Had the woman some psionic gift of her own, that let her see into his heart? Or was she just unusually perceptive? "I have become bitter of late," he admitted.

Allouene nodded with satisfaction. "You have seen too much of human selfishness and self-seeking. But we try to use those urges, to channel them into some sort of system that makes people protect the rights of everyone, in order to protect their own interests."

Magnus frowned. "An interesting goal. Have you ever succeeded?"

"Never perfectly," Allouene admitted, "but we have managed to harness self-interest into workable systems again and again. We console ourselves with the thought that no system can be perfect, and we have made progress."

"Fascinating," Magnus murmured, holding himself very carefully. All his own near-despair, his disgust with his relatives, his disillusionment in discovering how few people really seemed to care for anyone else's good—it all came together and stabbed, white-hot, toward an organization that was at least *trying* to put ideals into action. But some lingering caution made him say, "I should think you would find a great number of recruits."

Allouene's expression showed some bitterness of her own. "It would be wonderful—but very few people seem to be interested in working toward anyone's welfare but their own. Of those who are, many of them aren't strong enough, either emotionally or physically, to last through our training. The rewards, after all, are only in knowing that you have left a world better off than you found it—and we aren't even always successful in that."

"You must have been recruiting for a long time, to have seen enough cases to generalize," Magnus said.

"Every time I put together a new mission team," Allouene assured him. "When we are appointed Mission Leaders, you see, we are given the responsibility of finding our own agents, of recruiting them and training them."

Magnus stared. "You mean that if I join SCENT, I will be working with you?"

"After your training," Allouene said, "yes."

And that, of course, decided the matter.

CHAPTER
~6~

Ian froze. Then, before he could catch up his staff and bolt, the man smiled and laughed. It was a warm, friendly laugh, and Ian relaxed a little. Surely the man could not be an enemy if he behaved in so friendly a fashion. Besides, he wore no livery; he could not be a keeper, or any other servant of Lord Murthren—at least, no more than anyone was. He was a broad-shouldered man, and his arms and legs were thick with muscles. Ian could see this easily, for he wore a tight-fitting jerkin and leggings. His body looked very hard underneath the gray, belted tunic, and his leggings were so smooth they might have been a lord's hose. His black hair was cut short, no longer than his collar. His face was craggy, with a long, straight nose and lantern jaw. His eyes were large, but above them, his brows seemed knit in a perpetual frown. It was a harsh face, and grim—but when he smiled, as he did now, it turned into friendliness. Somehow, Ian felt he could not fear such a man, or had no cause to—this, in spite of the sword that hung belted at his hip, and the dagger across from it. These, and his short hair, told Ian the man's profession, as surely as though it had been written on his forehead. He was a free-lance, a soldier who wandered about the country and sold his services to whatever lord needed him that month. He was not a serf, but a gentleman, free to travel where he wished, as long as he did not offend the great lords. His boots came up to his calves and had high, thick heels—a horseman, then. But where was his horse?

Dead, of course—or the property of some lord. Like as not, he owned no mount of his own, but rode whatever nag was given him by the nobleman who employed him. He might leave, but the horse would stay.

"Look carefully before you drink," he said to Ian, "and listen more closely. If you had, you would have heard me step up to the stream and sit down." Then he frowned, and Ian shrank back from the sudden grimness of his face. "What are you doing, out here in the middle of the forest, alone at night? Your parents will be worried."

Ian heaved a sigh of relief. This soldier did not even know that his parents were dead, so he could not have been sent here to search for a runaway serf boy.

The soldier was looking impatient. "Come, boy— how is it you are out here late, and alone?"

"I . . ." Ian bit his lip. "I came out to . . . to gather nuts." He didn't even sound convincing to himself.

Nor to the free-lance. "So late at night?"

"It was this morning, sir," Ian improvised. "But I lost my way, and try as I would to find my home, I think I'm even further lost. So I have no idea where I am, or where my home is."

The free-lance scowled, like a thundercloud. "You are a very poor liar," he said severely. Suddenly, he smiled again. "Well, I am properly served. It is no business of mine, why you are out here—and if you lie about it, you seem to feel no need of my help to get home again." He looked Ian over, puzzled. "Too young to have a brand on you. Still, there is no doubt you are a serf's son. If the soldiers catch you here, late and alone at night, it will go hard with you." He seemed to come to a decision, and stood. Ian stared up at him, awed, for the process of standing seemed to go on and on as the man unfolded and expanded. He was a giant, or at least, much taller than any man Ian had ever seen!

He held out a hand. "Walk with me, then, boy, and I'll be your protection from them. You are my apprentice, accompanying me to polish my armor and mend my clothes."

Ian seized the hand with relief and gladness—here was a friend where he had least expected to find one, his passport out of the forest and to safety.

But . . .

"Sir," he said, "will the foresters believe it?"

The free-lance smiled. "It is rare, true. Few blank-shield soldiers would wish to burden themselves with a child. Still, it is not unknown, and when we've come out of the forest, I will buy you some

111

clothes that befit your new station. We will say that you are my nephew."

But Ian remembered that the soldiers who were looking for him would scarcely believe such a tale—and that they were still looking for a young serf boy who had run away.

It was almost as though the soldier heard his thoughts. "There were foresters and soldiers thick about here just now. Like as not, they were hunting for you. They would scarcely believe such a tale." He nodded, agreeing with himself. "Yes. We had better go quickly, then, boy, and very quietly, by back trails. What have you done, that they should search for you by night in this wilderness?"

Ian's heart leaped into his throat—but he swallowed, and forced himself to speak. What could he say, except the truth? Anything else would be to abuse this new-found friend. If he chose to have nothing to do with a runaway, well, then Ian was no worse off than before—but if he found it out later, then he might betray Ian to the foresters in anger. "I have escaped, sir." Not all the truth, perhaps, but enough.

And the soldier seemed satisfied. He nodded and said, "Come, then. I know what it is, to escape—and be found."

Ian looked up, startled at his tone—but the freelance was no longer smiling, nor looking at him. He was gazing straight ahead, frowning—and remembering.

• • •

Basic training was a crashing bore. Magnus couldn't understand why the other recruits complained so much—ten-mile hikes in the middle of the night were an inconvenience, of course, but nothing he hadn't had to do at home, now and then. Learning to ride was no problem for a young man who had virtually grown up on horseback, though his city-bred companions had quite a few choice words to say about the hardness of their saddles as they were learning to post. He became used to hearing them grumble, "Where are the brakes on this thing?" and, "Show him who's boss, she says! Confounded beast *knows* who's boss, no matter who's in the saddle!"

Magnus had the good sense to keep his mouth shut when the instructor was teaching them how to pitch camp, and did pick up a few useful tricks without giving in to the impulse to mention a few of his own. He went on keeping his mouth shut while Svenson, the grizzled old field agent who was in charge of martial arts, gave them a ritual dressing-down and challenge before he began teaching them.

"Ed Gar!" he snorted as he passed Magnus, checking his name from the list. He looked him up and down, mostly up, and said, "Gar Pike, more likely, as long as you are, and with that length of jaw!"

Magnus didn't respond, recognizing the gambit of insult, to make him know his place. Svenson eyed him hungrily, hoping for indignation, for a challenge to put down, but didn't get it, and only sighed as he turned away to the next recruit, shaking his head.

Then he gave them a brief lecture about martial

arts, telling them why they wore such outlandish uniforms for practice, and how the color of the belt denoted the level of their skill, which was why theirs were white. To his credit, he told them a little of the philosophy underlying it, too, though it was mostly as a guide to how to defeat an attacker.

Then he put them through their paces in unarmed combat. Magnus dutifully mimicked every move the man made, duplicated every sequence of blows, but forgot to do it clumsily at first, and the veteran pulled him aside at the end of the second session. "Done this before, haven't you?"

"I didn't think it showed," Magnus answered.

"When you do every move exactly right the first time? You bet it shows! What belt do you hold?"

Magnus could have claimed to be a belted knight, which was true, but he knew it wasn't quite what the man had in mind. "None."

"No belt?" Svenson frowned—up, of course. He was a foot shorter than Magnus, though just as heavily built, and almost as fast. "Your instructor's guilty of gross negligence! What school did you go to?"

"None, for martial arts," Magnus said.

Svenson's frown deepened. "Where'd you learn it, then?"

"From my father, as I grew up."

Svenson turned away, looking exasperated, and nodded. "Yep, that explains it, all right. Here I am, trying to teach these lunkheads something that you took for granted. I don't suppose he ever took you to competition?"

Magnus knew he was speaking of formal tournaments, not actual combat. "No. We lived very far out in the . . . boondocks." The word was unfamiliar, but he managed to remember it.

"Too far to go to the nearest tournament, eh? What did he teach you? Kung fu? Karate? Jujitsu?"

Magnus stared, then spread his hands, at a loss. "He taught me to fight."

"A little bit of everything," Svenson interpreted, "all rolled together into a system that can take on any of them—which is just what I'm teaching you. No, cancel that—what I'm teaching the rest of these would-be heroes. Maybe I oughta have you join the teaching staff."

Magnus picked his words with care. "By your leave, sir, that might be damaging to morale."

Svenson gave him an approving glance. "Yes, it might, and it might set them all against you, too. Good point, Gar Pike. We'll just keep on as we're going, shall we? With you pretending you don't know anything—and who knows, you might pick up a few new techniques."

"Yes, sir," Magnus agreed. "I'll try to be a bit more clumsy from now on."

He wasn't the only one who already knew martial arts, but the other had much better sense than to let it show. His name was Siflot, and he was wiry and nimble, but pretended to be clumsy. He had a marvelous sense of humor, though, and every trip, every stumble, brought laughter from those around him. Siflot always came up grinning, which Magnus at first ascribed to good sportsmanship, but eventually realized was satisfaction—Siflot had intended to get a laugh, and was grinning because he had succeeded.

During the first evening, though, he stepped aside from the campfire, took three balls out of his pockets, and began to juggle. Conversation gradually stilled as the other recruits watched him, waiting for a fumble, a dropped ball—but it never came. Finally, Siflot caught all three balls and tucked them away, turning back to the campfire—and noticed all eyes on him. He laughed, embarrassed. "I have to practice every day, that's all, or I'll lose my touch." He sat down by the fire.

"I can see why you'd want to keep it, a skill like that," Ragnar said.

"That could be useful in a medieval society," Lancorn added.

"It's an old skill," Siflot admitted, smiling at her. She smiled back with a slumbrous look, but it seemed to go right past Siflot; he turned back to the fire, asking Ragnar, "What tricks do the jugglers do, in your home?"

The conversation picked up again, but Magnus gazed at Siflot, weighing him. He certainly had intended his mates to notice his skill, though Magnus didn't doubt he did need to stay in practice—and if he could juggle like that, he certainly couldn't be as clumsy as he pretended. No, more—deliberately taking pratfalls like his required a great deal of skill and control over his body. Why, Magnus wondered, was he playing the fool?

He had his answer in the others' reactions to Siflot. Within days, everyone liked him—and were a

little condescending. Everyone knew that Siflot
could never be a threat—which meant that if he ever
did need to fight one of them, he would have the advantage of tremendous surprise. In the meantime, he
had become everyone's friend and everyone's
confidant—there was no one who didn't trust Siflot.
Why not? He could never hurt them.

But Magnus had a different notion of the matter,
and the second day, he managed to pair up with Siflot
in unarmed combat class. True to his promise to
Svenson, he did his best to be clumsy, stumbling as
often as Siflot and falling down in the middle of a
throw just as he did. The climax of the day came
when they both kicked at each other at the same moment, and both missed. Siflot laughed, and Magnus
grinned, then stepped in for a hip-throw and stumbled, giving Siflot the perfect opportunity to pin him
with an elbow-lock, which the juggler dutifully
did—then skidded in his own turn, and landed right
beside Magnus, who looked over at him, grinned,
and said with all the sarcasm he could muster,
"White belt, *sure*."

A wary look flickered over Siflot's face, then was
swallowed in an impish grin. "Why, Gar Pike, how
could I be anything else?"

Svenson stamped up to spare Magnus an answer.
"If you two clowns are through with the circus now,
we might get on with the lesson."

"Oh yes, sir! Yes, sir!" Siflot rolled up to his feet,
nodding—no, bobbing. "It was the hip-throw, wasn't
it, sir?" And he grabbed Magnus and executed the
move perfectly—except that when Magnus was at

the top of the arc, Siflot collapsed. Magnus couldn't help it—he burst into laughter as he rolled off Siflot, then caught the smaller man's shoulder, asking, "Are you all right?"

Siflot came up grinning. "Why, of course, friend Pike—you landed as a feather would." Then, to Svenson, "I'm learning, sir."

"Sure are," Svenson growled. "Pretty soon, maybe you won't fall until he hits the ground. A little more effort and a little less humor, Siflot." He turned away, fighting to keep his face straight.

They faced off again. Siflot asked, "And how old were you when you took your black belt, friend Pike?"

"I never did," Magnus answered. "We don't use them."

"Ah. Suspenders, no doubt."

"No, garters. Think you can stay on your feet this time, friend Siflot?"

"No, friend Pike, but I might stay on yours."

They all called him "Pike" by the third day, following Svenson's lead. Ragnar claimed the name suited him.

Siflot kept the classes from being boring, with his mock clumsiness and wide-eyed innocence that led him to ask the most hilarious questions. Still, Svenson was only teaching Magnus what he already knew, and he had to summon all his patience to take them with good grace.

But the acculturation classes were another matter, partly because it was material he didn't know at all—the background, social system, and customs of the world he was being sent to—and partly because Allouene was teaching them. Soaking up the history, dialect, and laws of a new planet was fascinating, and watching Allouene was a pleasure that Magnus felt to his marrow, even though she was all business as she paced before the class, with nothing seductive or alluring in her manner. But the honey of her hair still shone, her eyes flashed as she told them about the inequities of the aristocratic system, and her movements were poetry.

Apparently, Magnus's heart was not locked up quite as tightly as he had thought—but even if it had been, the rest of his body was not. Watching Allouene roused physical sensations that permeated Magnus's whole body, even though his emotions stirred only slightly.

Of course, he feigned a relaxed posture and kept his face impassive, showing none of what he felt.

"We'll begin by telling you why we're going," she said, "and the answer is that the agent in charge has called for help."

"I thought SCENT didn't like to send in lots of agents," Ragnar said.

Allouene nodded, making her hair sway around her face in a way that Magnus found enchanting. "SCENT rules are very strict about disrupting indigenous cultures, and the fewer agents involved, the less the chance of disruption. The ideal is to send in one agent only, and have him put the planet on the road to democracy single-handed—but that almost never happens."

The words transfixed Magnus—for that was exactly what his father had done: come to Gramarye as an agent of SCENT and set it on the road to democracy, single-handed. Well, not by himself, no, but without calling in any other SCENT agents. He made do with local talent—very well: he married one, and raised some others.

Of course, that was unjust. Magnus knew quite well that Rod Gallowglass had stayed on Gramarye because he had fallen in love with Magnus's mother. He knew it not just from his parents' report, but from several others of the older generation who had witnessed it—including Fess. And anything the children had done had been incidental.

Until now.

"Usually the scout agent calls for help," Allouene went on, "just as he has in this case. His name is Oswald Majorca, and he has set up a thriving business as a merchant, which allows him to travel anywhere he wants, even to other continents. It also gives him an excuse to send his own agents to any other city, and they might 'just happen' to stop over at any place in between. He has situated himself admirably, and given us a great start. It's up to us not to blow it for him."

Allouene turned to key the display screen to a diagram of a solar system, showing a yellow sun tinged with orange. "It's a G-type star, but it's cooler than Sol, so even though the planet's only the second one out and is closer to its sun than Terra is to Sol, it has about the same temperature range. It has three continents—the largest has an inland sea—and a host of islands. Serfs flee to those islands now and then, so the lords have to mount expeditions to clean them out periodically."

"They could just leave them alone," Lancorn objected.

There were only the four of them in this class—presumably, Allouene was keeping her mission small. Magnus was glad to see that Siflot was one of the four.

"Of course the lords could leave them alone," Allouene agreed, "but they aren't about to. The official exuse is to eliminate piracy—but they also, incidentally, wipe out any possibility that somebody besides the ruling elite might have a decent life, and make sure that the serfs don't go getting ideas about rising above their station. There's a pocket of escaped serfs growing to the critical point right now, on an island they've named Castlerock . . ." An island toward the northern coast of the inland sea began to glow. ". . . and the lords are getting ready for a full-scale expedition. They've already sent a small band, but the serfs killed off the officers and persuaded the soldiers to join them."

"Dangerous," Siflot murmured, and Lancorn looked at him in surprise.

"The lords think so, too," Allouene agreed. "That's why they're preparing the big expedition—but I'm getting ahead of myself. Back to the basics. History next."

Her four students keyed their notebook displays to the topic.

"This all started seven hundred years ago, when the government of the Terran Sphere was still the Interstellar Dominion Electorates. A thousand or so financiers set up the planet as a tax haven. They had the arrogance and audacity to name it just that—Taxhaven. They were ready for retirement, so they found an undeveloped world and bought it outright. Then they shipped in all the machinery necessary for a luxurious life-style, and each declared it to be the permanent site of residence for his or her whole family. They left their sons and daughters on Terra to look after business."

Ragnar raised a hand. "But wouldn't they still have come under the Terran tax laws?"

"Technically, no," Allouene said, "and the technicalities were exactly what their lawyers went to court with. The financiers gave up their citizenship and declared themselves to be a sovereign government, so they didn't have to pay tax to the I.D.E."

"The businesses would still have been taxed," Ragnar objected.

"Their accountants arranged things so that the businesses were either operating at a loss, or showing so little profit that it didn't matter—not hard, when all the real profits were going to Taxhaven."

"The I.D.E. allowed that kind of gold flow outside its boundaries?" Lancorn asked, amazed.

"No—the younger generation officially sent all the profits to their parents' Terran accounts, which were only nominally taxed, since the older generation were foreign citizens. Of course, the 'kids' had the use of their parents' mansions and yachts, and were paid excellent salaries for pocket money—but officially, they were just hired help."

"Neat," Ragnar said sourly. "Very neat."

Magnus had trouble following it all; where he came from, you paid what tax you were told, or you went to prison. He made a note to look up Terran tax laws.

"Didn't the second generation feel as though they were getting short shrift?" Lancorn asked.

"No—they knew their day was coming, and in the meantime, they were enjoying power and privilege. When they reached retirement age and grew weary of the fleshpots of Terra, they moved to Taxhaven and left the third generation to take care of business on Terra and the inner planets."

"Of course, they had been waiting in demure patience for their turn at power," Siflot murmured.

"Very good, Siflot," Allouene said, with surprised approval. "I thought you'd never say anything. Gar, you might work on that, too. No, the grandchildren had been fuming at not being the big cheeses, so they didn't mind being left holding the moneybag when Poppa and Momma wanted to retire to the boondocks."

"Then Poppa and Momma could champ at the bit." The idiom came easily to Magnus, and he was probably the only one there who understood what it really meant.

"A word to the wise was sufficient." Allouene gave Magnus a slow smile. "Will you always do as I bid you?"

Magnus felt the thrill pass through him, and give her a smile in return. "Always awaiting your 'come hither,' Madame."

She turned back to the screen with a self-satisfied smile, and Magnus felt the danger pass, though the thrill still vibrated within him. "You're right about the second generation," Allouene said, "but when Grandma and Grandpa finally died, the fortune officially stayed on Taxhaven, and the second generation became the dukes and marquises and counts. Then the third generation retired and moved up to take over the estates and fortunes, while the fourth took over the business—and so it went."

"And the government never caught on to them?" Lancorn asked, outraged.

"They caught on right away, but there was a limit to how much they could do about it. As the generations passed, the government put increasing pressure on Taxhaven to become an official dominion, part of the I.D.E., and therefore subject to the same tax laws as the rest of the Terran planets, but Taxhaven adamantly refused, and had the Sol-side lawyers and lobbyists to be able to prevent a takeover. Their lobbyists and tame Electors were also able to keep the I.D.E. from boosting taxes on Solar System earnings much past five percent, and to frustrate every other strategem the Executive Secretary of the I.D.E. could think of."

"There had to be a limit to that kind of influence," Ragnar said, frowning. "I thought the I.D.E. turned to a rob-from-the-rich, give-to-the-masses program toward the end."

Allouene nodded. "During the last, dark days of the I.D.E., the rabble-rousing Electors of the LORDS party rammed through legislation forcing the Taxhaven barons to pay their back taxes. The move gained them a lot of support from the masses, but the Taxhaven families had just finished selling off all their holdings. They retired to the 'home planet' *en masse*—except for those family members who were also in the LORDS party, making sure that no matter which way fortune fell, the Taxhaven families would prosper. These members were instrumental in the *coup d'état* that finally buried the I.D.E. and set up the Proletarian Eclectic State of Terra, which cut off contact with the outer, and unprofitable, planets—including Taxhaven."

"Alas!" Siflot wiped away an imaginary tear. "That must have broken all their clinking hearts!"

No one laughed, but everyone's lips quirked in amusement. Allouene smiled broadly and nodded. "It couldn't have worked out better for them."

"Meaning it was their offspring who set it up," Ragnar interpreted.

"Certainly they supported the idea. After all, it was in perfect accord with the wishes of the Taxhaven artistocracy, as they termed themselves— they had officially cut off communication with Terra from their end, anyway. So the families relaxed and lolled back among their local riches, and devoted themselves to every pleasure they could think of, while their younger members saw to it that they still received their dividends from all the Terran-sphere companies in which they owned stock."

Lancorn frowned. "I thought you said they had been cut off from Terra."

"Only officially," Siflot said.

Christopher Stasheff

"Very good," Allouene said. "Yes, there was still a tiny but constant stream of communication with Terra and its richer colonies—unofficial, clandestine, technically illegal, but carefully protected by wealth and privilege at both ends of the line. It sent not only money, but also every luxury the Terran planets could boast, and every new one that was invented. This even included a few items of state-of-the-art technology, but not many."

"I thought they wanted every luxury they could think of," Ragnar said.

"Perhaps," Magnus murmured, "but they did not want to have to look at the technology that produced it."

Allouene looked up sharply. "You sound as though you know, Gar."

Magnus felt the tension, so he shrugged very casually. "I've seen people like that."

"Well, you're right." Allouene was eyeing him in a new light. "The founding families had decided that the most graceful and elegant age of Terra's history had been the late Seventeenth Century, the age of Charles the Second and Louis the Fourteenth, of the Drury Lane Theater and the Three Musketeers, and had devoted themselves to living with all the luxuries of that age but none of the inconveniences. They dressed in their own versions of 1670's clothing, took the waters at spas, attended reproductions of Restoration theaters, rode horses and drove in carriages, flocked to each other's balls, and paraded in their own court masques."

"Very pretty," Magnus murmured. "I understand

126

the real seventeenth century had its share of filth and sickness, though."

"Let us not be *too* historically accurate," Siflot said softly.

Allouene laughed with them, then nodded. "Yes, they wanted limits—renovation, not restoration. Modern medicine banished the specter of disease that had so ravished the real Seventeenth Century, and modern building materials prevented a re-creation of the Great Fire of London. Their carriages rode on hidden anti-gravity units that cushioned the jarring of springless iron wheels, and modern weapons guaranteed their safety."

"Safety?" Magnus frowned. "From whom? Are there ferocious animals you have not told us about?"

Allouene shook her head, and her golden mane swirled prettily, almost making Magnus miss the next few words. "Anything that looked like a dangerous predator had been annihilated when they first arrived, except for a few specimens kept in zoo-parks as curiosities."

"What else was there to fear?" Lancorn demanded, but she looked as though she didn't want to know.

"What else?" Allouene repeated, with a grim smile. "What was the Restoration without Nell Gwyn? Who was going to perform in their theaters? Who would warm their beds when they wished to be naughty, who would shift the scenes . . . ?"

"Who would grow the food?" Magnus murmured.

"Robots could do that," Ragnar protested.

"Of course," Lancorn agreed, "but who would cook it?"

"Again, robots!"

Allouene nodded. "Robots could have done it—
but it was so much more satisifactory to have a living cook to scold and threaten. In fact, when you
really get right down to it, one of the greatest pleasures of the aristocracy has always been having peasants to lord it over and kick around, and wait upon
you hand and foot."

Magnus sat immobile. He couldn't quite claim innocence, but he had always been angry with lords
who mistreated their people. He'd even done something about it, once or twice—personally.

"The ladies needed maids to help them dress and
undress, after all," Allouene went on, "and the men
needed valets. The land needed tenants to care for it,
and living human beings were so much more aes-
thetic than soulless robots."

"So they brought slaves," Lancorn growled.

"Serfs," Allouene corrected. "They're tied to the
soil—even if the land changes hands, they don't.
They stay on the estate. The one good thing about it
is that they can't be bought and sold."

"The *only* good thing," Lancorn snorted.

"Where did they get them?" Ragnar growled.

"The original would-be aristocrats each recruited
a hundred ordinary people who badly needed
money," Allouene told them. "Some were horribly
in debt to the founders, some were chronic gamblers,
some were alcoholics and drug addicts, some were
poor, some wanted enough money to have families.
All were seduced by the offer of a lifetime's income
in return for five years' service on a new world, the

salary to be held in a Terran bank for them, earning interest until their return. A hundred recruits for each plutocrat, a hundred who gladly agreed to come along—or sometimes reluctantly, not that it mattered."

"A hundred thousand serfs in the making," Lancorn said, paling.

Magnus sat frozen. Was this how the peasants of his own world of Gramarye had been recruited—with lies and coercion? But no—he remembered; Father Marco Ricci had left records, and Magnus's parents had gone back in time and talked with people who had been there. The ancestors of Gramarye's people had volunteered, and gladly—they had been trying to escape the depersonalized society that had evolved with high technology. No doubt they hadn't realized how their descendants would live—but people seldom thought things through to the end.

Including himself?

For the first time, Magnus wondered what he was getting himself into.

"Why didn't they leave when their five years were up?" Siflot asked, but from the tone of his voice, he had already guessed.

"Because they couldn't," Ragnar snorted.

"They never came back, of course," Lancorn agreed. "How could they, if their lords didn't want them to? Who owned the spaceships, who controlled the police?" She looked to Allouene for confirmation.

The lieutenant nodded. "The hundred thousand were immediately locked into serfdom, and never came out of it. Moreover, the lords demanded that they have families, and there weren't very many of them who had the strength to risk the punishments waiting for anyone who disobeyed. The few who held out were tortured, and caved in quickly—especially since the very few who refused to give in in spite of the pain, died in the process."

"So the lords were sure they wouldn't run out of servants," Lancorn said, her face stony.

"The next generation was guaranteed," Allouene said, "and the first batch of rebellious genes had been weeded out. The second generation of serfs grew up with the habit of obedience, and learned how to swallow their anger—and outrage and rebellion."

"Weren't there any who couldn't quench the fires?" Siflot asked softly.

"Of course," Allouene said. "In every generation a few rebelled—and were hanged, or drawn and quartered, or killed in battle. No matter which way, over the generations, their genes were weeded out.

"But other genes were reinforced."

Ragnar frowned, puzzled; Lancorn cocked her head to the side, finger to her cheek; but Magnus just sat rigidly, and Siflot stared in horror. "Of course!" he cried. "Only a hundred thousand! Inbreeding!"

Allouene nodded. "A hundred thousand isn't a very large gene pool, after all, and after a few generations, no matter who you married, he or she was probably related to you, one way or another. By the tenth generation, they *definitely* were, no 'probably' about it—and recessive gene reinforced recessive gene. The consequences of inbreeding began to appear: loss of intelligence, dwarfism, giantism, hemophilia—and mental illness. Coupled with genius sometimes, other times with idiocy, sometimes all by itself—but madness nonetheless."

"They had to have known," Ragnar growled. "The original lords must have known what they were doing to the future generations."

But Magnus shook his head. "Why should they have thought it through? They didn't care."

"But they should have cared about their own descendants!" Lancorn turned to Allouene. "It hit them too, didn't it?"

Allouene nodded. "Not as fast as among the serfs, nor as badly—they always had a steady stream of new blood trickling in from Terra, after all—but they did have occasional outbreaks. Far more often, it showed up among the gentry."

"Gentry?" Ragnar asked. "Did they coerce some bourgeois into coming along, too?"

"No," Allouene said. "They made them locally."

Ragnar shook his head, missing the reference. "Where did they come from?"

"Oh, Ragnar!" Lancorn snapped. "Don't be any more dense than you have to be!"

Ragnar glowered at her. "Maybe I'm just too naive. Spell it out for me, O wise one."

"Well," she answered, "what do you think is going to happen when a lord brings in a buxom serf wench to warm his bed?"

Ragnar froze.

"There will be a child who looks remarkably like that lord," Siflot said softly.

Allouene nodded, her face hard. "Occasionally, a bastard might result from a lady's inviting some strapping, handsome young serf in for the night, but far less frequently than the lords' by-blows—it was a rare noblewoman who wanted to go through nine months of pregnancy ending in labor, for a peasant man. Far more often, the ladies, like the lords, only wanted pleasure, not more children. The lords could have used birth control medications of their own with their peasant wenches, of course, but they wanted to increase the population. Why not? The more there were, the more servants they had."

"After all," Magnus murmured, "a lord's valet should be a gentleman, not a serf, should he not?"

Allouene frowned, even as she nodded. "You sound as if you know, Gar. But you're right—and the steward of the estate should be better-born than the average laborer, and there was a need for lawyers, and for clerks to handle the drudgery of the trickle of trade, and to oversee the building of new houses and the laying out of new gardens, and to act in the theaters. . . ."

"So a class of petty aristocracy came into being," Ragnar interpreted.

Allouene shook her head. "Gentry aren't noble, Ragnar—the lords make a very big point of that. They're a middle class, between the serfs and the nobility. In Europe, they came from the knights and the squires, and from the merchants; on Taxhaven, they've been given the same jobs, if not the titles. But they've developed their own pedigrees and mores anyway. They've never owned land legally, but when the same family of gentry has been in charge of the same hundred acres for three generations, it creates the illusion of ownership, and certainly a tie to the land. They're allowed to earn money and save it in their own right, and are comfortably well-off, even sometimes wealthy in a small way. They resent their neglectful parent class, of course, but nonetheless, they side with the lords against the serfs, more or less automatically—they have something to lose, after all. Of course, there are always new gentlemen coming into being, not of the established families, and they're scorned and looked down upon, and only allowed to marry one of the new gentlewomen—but their children are accepted, so the class keeps increasing in number. They're the middle-rank officers in the army, the mid-level managers on the estates, the tax collectors and magistrates and squires. They're resented by the serfs, and resent the lords in their own turn—but each class knows its place, and knows the painful, even lethal, penalties for stepping out of that place, so the society endures, though not happily."

So they were bound for a planet governed by grown-up spoiled brats who intended to stay that way, lording it over a population of serfs dressed in medieval simplicity and filth, with an intermediary class of gentry to take care of the day-to-day administration and the direct contact with the serfs.

Magnus could see why Allouene had decided they needed changing.

CHAPTER
~7~

The free-lance asked, "Can you move quietly, in the wood?"

Ian tried to smile. "I can try."

"Well, then, let's away." The soldier turned to go, then stopped and looked back over his shoulder. "I cannot go on calling you 'boy,' " he said. "It's too clumsy. What's your name?"

More danger—but Ian was in the thick of it now. He might as well pray for the best and tell the truth. "Ian," he said. "Son of Tobin."

"And I am Gar Pike." The free-lance smiled. "Well, then, Ian Tobinson—let's away."

They went onward under the trees, between the trunks, Gar as silent as the wind and almost as silent as the dwarves in his soft boots. Ian plucked up his courage and followed.

They threaded their way through the back trails, so faint that Ian could barely make them out. Every now and then, Gar would stop, cock his head, and listen. Then he would nod and lead Ian forth. Several times, though, when he stopped to listen, he turned quickly into the nearest thicket, parting the bushes before him and stepping into their center, holding the bushes back for Ian to follow, then pressing them back together and crouching down, motioning for Ian to do likewise and pressing a finger to his lips for silence. When this happened, Ian would do as Gar bade him and stay very still, breathing through his mouth. Then, after a while, he would hear the crashing and the crunching of the soldiers as they moved nearer. Several times they came almost to the thickets where Gar and Ian were hiding and Ian would hear them talking. They were afraid the lord would punish them for not having found the runaway youth. Each time this happened, Ian's body knotted with fear. Not so much as he had felt before—he did not panic; Gar would protect him, he knew, if it came to a fight. Ian saw his own hands tighten on his quarterstaff, though, and remembered very well that Gar was, after all, only one man. If he had to fight trained soldiers, perhaps he would not be able to prevail. If that happened, Ian resolved to guard his back for him. Though he was only a boy against full-grown men, he knew his quarterstaff-play well, and might be able to delay a second soldier long enough for Gar to finish with the first.

They travelled through the forest all night in this fashion, and the near brushes with the soldiers became less frequent. But near dawn, when they were about to hide for the day, Gar suddenly turned aside from the trail. "Take cover, and quickly!"

Ian leaped after him, pushing through some underbrush into the center of a thicket. There they crouched on the bare earth, for all the world like deer. "Down," Gar murmured, though he himself only sat, "and be very still."

There was more tension in him than usual. Ian huddled under the leaves, wondering what was so much more dangerous this time.

Then he heard three voices. One of them was a cutting nasal whine—and Ian's heart raced, for he recognized it. "If we do not find him, serfs, the hide on your back will be scored!"

"But, my lord . . ." The soldier sounded exhausted. "We have searched all night, we have searched all over the wood. Surely one of the other bands will have found him by now."

"Impossible," the other soldier snapped. Then, in a placating tone, "It is our duty to our Lord Murthren to search for the boy until we drop in our tracks, if need be."

My lord Murthren! It was well the soldiers did not find them then, for Ian could not have moved a hand or a foot. He was frozen, frozen with fear.

Gar cocked his head to the side, listening, interested.

"Well said, though fawning," the nasal voice sneered. "Now get on and do your job, and search for him!"

Ian trembled, recognizing Lord Murthren's voice.

The lord snapped, "You would be wiser to die

searching for him, than to suffer my displeasure. He has violated one of the Sacred Places of the Old Ones! If we do not find and slay him, a curse, a murrain, shall fall upon all my land, my domains!"

Ian's eyes widened with fear. A murrain, a dread disease, spreading over all the whole duchy! Cattle wasting away and dropping dead in the fields—perhaps people, too! He bowed his head, and squeezed his eyes shut against tears as the feeling of guilt within him grew, gaining strength. "One of the Sacred Places of the Old Ones"—was that the strange "Safety Base" into which he had strayed? And how, then, did Milord Murthren know of it?

But the voices faded away. When Ian could no longer hear them, he started to get up—but Gar's hand fell on his shoulder, holding him in place. Ian froze, then looked questioningly at Gar. The freelance laid a finger across his lips again, head cocked to listen.

Perhaps ten minutes longer they stayed in their places. Then Gar rose slowly, and Ian, with a sigh of thanks, rose with him. His legs tingled as the blood flowed back into them. He stretched sore, stiff muscles, then looked up to find Gar gazing down at him quizzically. "So that was your crime! 'One of the Sacred Places of the Old Ones'! That great stone egg in the center of the meadow—was that it?"

Ian nodded, unable to speak.

Gar chuckled, shaking his head. "What superstitious fools, to fear such places!" he said. "Though I'm sure the lords cultivate the rumor. I know someone who sheltered in an Old Ones' place himself once, when his side lost the battle and the enemy was searching for him. He told me that the guardian spirits the Old Ones left are gentle to those who claim their protection—and if they laid a curse upon him, it was a strange one, for he lived well, and longer than many soldiers I have known."

He looked about him, sniffing. "I smell dawn coming." He turned away. "Come, Ian! We must be out of this forest before the sun rises."

Ian looked after him, then stumbled into a run until he caught up with Gar. His legs seemed leaden with exhaustion, but if the free-lance could push on, so could he. And within him, there was relief—if Gar had said it, it must be true. He need not fear the curse, nor the murrain upon Milord Murthren's domain.

They came out onto the roadway as the sun peeked over the hills, and the sky was streaked with rose and gold. Gar looked around him, breathing deeply of the scents of the morning, then looked down at Ian. "We are nearly to the end of our journey," he said. "Half a mile down this road is a town, and I know a man there who will shelter us and ask no questions." He smiled, warm and friendly. "Let your head lie easy, my lad. Once you are dressed in my livery, no man will question you. You are twelve good miles from the edge of Lord Carnot Murthren's domains. In fact"—he chuckled—"they are apt to think you are still hiding in the forest, not far from wherever you entered it." He cocked his head to the side. "How long has it been since you ran away from your home?"

139

Ian started to answer, then stopped to think back. So much had happened . . . "Two days, sir. Two days, and two nights."

Gar nodded. "Yes, they will still think you are very close to home. Lord Murthren must have been searching beyond his own borders, out of sheer frustration. Whoever would believe a boy of twelve . . . Ten? Very well, ten . . . could forge his way through the whole of the forest, alone and at night?" He turned away, chuckling again and shaking his head. "Come, lad. Beds and hot porridge await us— nowhere nearly such excellent fare as you had in the Sacred Place of the Old Ones, no doubt, but nonetheless most welcome after a long night of walking."

Ian stumbled after him, sodden with fatigue, but with his heart lightened. Gar had proved that he had indeed spoken with a man who had been inside an Old Ones' place—for how else could he have known what lordly meals the guardian spirits prepared there?

Indeed, Magnus had spoken only the truth, though the man he had spoken of had been a merchant, not a soldier—Oswald Majorca. It had been one of the many anecdotes Master Oswald had related, to break the ice with his new agents while giving them some idea of the culture that had grown up on this outpost of inhumanity. But he had heard of the Safety Bases before that, from Allouene. She had finished up the briefing aboard ship—even in H-space, it took two weeks to reach Taxhaven.

That was two weeks together, with no one else to buffer personality clashes, and the cracks in the unit began to show. Ragnar was growing impatient with Allouene's occasional flirtations, especially since she never let him follow up, but always kept a wall of formality between them. Magnus kept the same kind of wall up from his side, too, so she spent larger portions of allure on him, the more so since, to all appearances, he wasn't responding—at least, not as much as she wanted.

Inside, though, he was, and it was driving him crazy, and by that, he knew her for a flawed leader. She was trying to bind her male agents to her by sexual attraction, not stopping to realize that she was creating rivalries that must sooner or later tear the group apart.

She was certainly tearing Magnus apart. He had to get away from the woman for a while—either that, or become very much closer; but whenever he thought about that last, something would slam shut within him, leaving him distanced from all emotions.

Lancorn was alert to every flirtation, every nuance, and resented it more and more with every day. Relations with her commander became very strained; they started being coldly polite to one another.

In short, Magnus expected them to be at each other's throats by the time they reached Taxhaven—as they probably would have, if it hadn't been for Siflot.

He always had a kind word for everyone, a comment that would make them all suddenly feel absurd to have been resentful, some quip or antic that would make tension explode in a burst of laughter. Siflot was the buffer, Siflot was the peacemaker—but by the time they dropped back into normal space and Taxhaven showed a discernible disk, even he was beginning to look frazzled. Magnus wasn't surprised—the chafing of others' emotions must have left him seriously abraded.

Siflot took refuge in playing his flute—a slender stalk that he carried hidden somewhere in his clothing. He hid himself away, either because it was a very private thing or because he knew that the lilting notes, sometimes shrill, could grate on others' nerves. Presumably he played in the privacy of his own cabin—no one would have known; the walls were soundproofed—but their cubicles were claustrophobic, so Magnus wasn't surprised, in his rambles through the bowels of the ship, to hear flute music drifting out of a darkened corridor now and again.

He rambled for the same reason that Siflot played music—to release tension, and to get away from the others for a little. He was sure Siflot felt the same needs, so whenever he heard the skipping notes coming out of the dark, he turned aside.

But as the disk that was Taxhaven swelled in their viewscreens, the thought of taking on a whole world began to make their personal conflicts seem unimportant, and they settled down for the last of the briefing.

"Why hasn't the D.D.T. done something about this place before now?" Lancorn demanded. "They've had more than a hundred years since they killed off PEST!"

"The Taxhaveners got to liking their life as petty

tyrants," Allouene explained, "and as the economy of PEST ground down under its reactionary, isolationist policies, the lords sold off all their Terran Sphere assets and moved everything to Taxhaven. The last few out did a very thorough job of burying the records—not hard to do, considering that there had been no official communication for five hundred years. The Interplanetary Police Force knew there was some kind of smuggling going on, but they were very firmly discouraged from pursuing it, so Taxhaven stayed buried in their files. The only trace of it was a standing joke that you've all probably heard gowing up—'I'll get so rich that I'll move to Taxhaven!' "

"Well, sure, I heard that." Lancorn frowned. "But I thought it just meant *a* tax haven."

"That's what we all thought," Allouene said grimly. "But when the D.D.T. revitalized the Interplanetary Police and expanded them to interstellar, one of the first things they did was to assign someone to go through all the dead files, looking for unfinished business. Fifteen years ago, she found the mention of Taxhaven. Ten years ago, SCENT finally worked through its agenda far enough to start searching for the planet. They assigned Oswald Majorca to the job—and five years ago, he found it. Last year, he finally admitted that he wasn't going to be able to handle it by himself and called for help."

"And we're it." Lancorn looked somber. "Just five of us and him, against a whole planet."

"Not the *whole* planet." Siflot looked pained. "Just a few thousand aristocrats."

"Seven thousand six hundred forty-two, as closely as we can count," Allouene said, "but you have to remember that there are about twenty thousand gentlemen and gentlewomen, who will side with the lords."

"I should think they could be made to see the advantages of democracy," Magnus murmured.

"Yes! Precisely, Gar!" Allouene beamed at him, and he felt it all the way to his toes. "If we can just make them see that they can be the ones who run things under a democracy, they'll start pushing for representation in councils!"

Magnus swam upstream against his yearning and said, "Then *they* will be the ones who oppress the serfs."

"Not if they're basing their democracy on universal principles." Allouene shook her head, and Magnus held his breath. "If they appeal for a voice in the government on the basis of basic human rights, they'll have to honor those same rights for the serfs. We just have to make sure they shift to that basis."

"So." Magnus frowned, suddenly freed from her spell by the grip of the problem confronting them. "Our strategy is to spread rumors about human rights. How are we to do that without subjecting anyone who mentions it to arrest and imprisonment?"

"By hiding it in a joke, or a story," Siflot answered, "so that the lords themselves are the ones who first spread it."

Allouene nodded. "Excellent idea. You were planning to be a strolling entertainer anyway, weren't you, Siflot?"

"All my life," the slender man murmured.

"I applaud you," Magnus said to Siflot, "but I am not suited to such tactics."

"You can repeat his stories and jokes, though, and tell them to other people," Allouene pointed out. "What kind of role can you find for yourself, in this kind of society?"

Magnus had been thinking that one over. "A mercenary, Lieutenant—a soldier of fortune."

"Good." Allouene nodded. "You can get close to the gentry that way—free-lance soldiers are *all* gentry, and they're hired as officers. You'll be in an ideal position to spread ideas, and even to get them up to the lords. But it's risky, you know."

Magnus nodded, not trusting himself to speak. Surely the woman must know the effect she had on his hormones, must know that she had supercharged him with the need for action! But, equally surely, she would show no sign of it. Yes, he might die, might be maimed—but he had to have action *now*, and he didn't see any way he could avoid the risk. "I'll call for help, if I need it," he promised.

Allouene nodded; she knew he was talking about the golden ship that was following them. She turned to Ragnar. "What role have you decided on, Ragnar?"

"A merchant." Ragnar shrugged. "I might as well make a few pieces of silver, while I'm at it."

"You'll work through Master Oswald, at first, then," Allouene said. She turned to Lancorn, and her voice became a little too casual. "What were you thinking of, Lancorn?"

"A gypsy," the woman said, staring levelly at the lieutenant. "The reports indicate that there are a few bands. The lords tolerate them for amusement."

"Descended from escaped serfs, probably," Allouene agreed, "but as you say, tolerated. A good idea."

"Ten minutes till we begin approach," the pilot's voice said from the intercom.

Allouene clapped her hands. "Enough! Ready or not, here we go! We'll land in the inland sea at night, on a bleak stretch of coastline. We'll row ashore, then strike out overland for Master Oswald's. He'll be there with a wagon and a cargo of trade goods. Lancorn, Siflot, and I will be merchants until we get to Master Oswald's; Ragnar and Gar will be our hired guards. Go pack your last few personal items, and web in!"

The landing craft was twice as good as its name—it brought them down in the water, then moved toward the shore with no sound other than the rippling of its wake, soon lost in the surf. When its bottom grated against sand, the forward hatch opened and the gangplank extruded. The five agents walked ashore without even getting their feet wet. Then the gangplank withdrew, the hatch closed, and the landing craft turned away and was lost in the night.

They turned and looked after it, somber, tense.

Siflot had the good sense not to try to relieve the tension.

Then a new star shot up from the sea and climbed into the sky. They watched it shrink, then disappear, trying to hold off the apprehension, the feeling of loneliness. They were committed now.

Then a golden star winked overhead and sailed by like a meteor—only it didn't fall, just kept on going. Magnus's heart warmed; before they had departed, Allouene had asked him to have his ship park in orbit, rather than trying to hide it on the surface. Magnus had given Herkimer instructions by radio—not that they were needed; Fess had already taught the robot about human thought-frequencies, modulation modes, and encoding, so Herkimer could hear his owner easily, if he thought hard enough. The reverse applied, too, of course, but Magnus didn't really think it would be necessary.

"We're here to stay, folks." Allouene turned to them, her grim face shadowed in the starlight. "From now on, our only help is each other." There wasn't the slightest trace of sexual allure about her now.

Then Siflot said, "I don't know how we'll ever last, all cooped up together on this planet."

The shout of laughter was much louder than the joke deserved, because it had been badly needed. The absurdity of their grating on each other's nerves with a whole planet to roam, compared to living in each other's laps as they had for the last two weeks, was hilarious—under the circumstances.

"Very good," Allouene said, smiling as they quieted. "But from now on we keep silent, until dawn. Let's go."

They trudged up the beach toward the boulders and marsh grass at its top. As they came up, a shadow detached itself from the rocks, and they all stopped, tensing, hands on their weapons.

"Good thing I'm on your side," the shadow said. "With that kind of noise, any guardsman within five kilometers could have heard you."

Allouene relaxed. "You gave me a start, Oswald. Agents, meet your Chief of Mission—Captain Oswald Majorca."

"*Master* Oswald, when any locals might be listening," the man said, extending a hand. He was short and very stocky—fat at first appearance, until you realized how much of it was muscle—and balding, with black hair around the sides. His face was round and snub-nosed, with quick, alert eyes. He clasped Lancorn's hand. "And you are Mistress . . . ?"

"Madame," Lancorn said, her voice brittle, but she took his hand. "Sheila Lancorn."

"Not 'Madame,' " Majorca corrected. "That's only for married female gentry, here. Aristocrats are addressed as 'milady.' Unmarried gentry, such as you are from now on, are 'Mistress.' Anything else, and you'll have the guardsmen on you for breaking the sumptuary laws." He released her hand and turned to Siflot. "And you are Master . . . ?"

"Siflot," the lean and lively one said, clasping his hand. "Do they call vagabonds 'Master' here?"

"A good point." Oswald looked him up and down in a quick glance. "And a travelling entertainer is an excellent cover—but it's risky; serfs of any kind can be clapped into prison at any moment, no reason given. You might want to have a gentleman-identity ready to hand. And you, Master . . . ?" He held his hand out to Ragnar.

"Ragnar Haldt," the big man said, returning the clasp, "and this is Gar Pike."

"Pleasure to meet you, Master Gar Pike." Oswald clasped Magnus's hand—and so it was fixed; Gar Pike he was, and Gar Pike he would remain.

"I've a wagon waiting. You can bunk in with a load of cloth." Oswald waved them on. "I piled it high around the edges and put muslin over the bales on the bottom, in case you wanted to sleep."

It was a tempting offer, but everybody was too tense—and too eager for a sight of their new world. They sat down among the bales, craning their necks to get a look at the night-veiled countryside as they passed. There wasn't much to see, since the moons had already set, but they could make out hedges, and the usual crazy-quilt pattern of fields of a medieval society, with the occasional dark blots that were peasant villages, and once, high up on a hilltop, a palace—but one that was surrounded by a curtain wall with crenellated towers. The thread of excited, whispered conversation ceased as they passed under the threat of that grim combination of pleasure and oppression—until Siflot murmured, "Could they be uncertain of the loyalty of their serfs?"

There was only a chuckle or two, until Magnus answered, "You've made your Marx." Then a real laugh sounded, though kept low, and conversation began again as they passed out of the shadow of the lord.

They came within sight of the town gate as the sun was sending in an advance guard of crimson rays. Master Oswald reined in his team and turned back to his passengers. "Down, now, all of you—I might be able to pass one of you off as a new factor and get him through the gates, but not a whole throng. I'm afraid it's going to be a while—fifteen minutes at least, then another fifteen from the gate to my shop. Stay low, and when the wagon starts to move again, don't breathe a word."

They lay down with some grumbling, and Allouene helped Oswald spread the tarpaulin over them and tie it down. After that, the conversation was muted, and restricted to such comments as, "Would you get your knee out of my ribs, Ragnar?" and "I never noticed what a lovely boot-sole you have, Pike!" "How come Allouene gets to stay out in the fresh air?" "Privileges of rank . . ."

Suddenly the wagon jerked into motion, and they all fell silent. The tension mounted as the wagon rolled.

Then they heard voices. "Ah, good morning, Master Oswald! Back from your journey, eh?"

"And what a lovely prize you've brought! Who would you be, Mistress, eh?"

"Mistress Allouene de Ville," Allouene answered, her voice slow, rich, and amused.

In the dim light under the tarp, Lancorn glowered, and Magnus realized that it wasn't just rank that had kept Allouene out in the open air. She could distract the gate-guards well enough so that they might not think to inspect the cargo.

"De Ville! Ah, have you brought back a devil, Master Oswald?"

"Best not to find out, Corporal," Oswald counselled. "She could set fire to more than your heart, I assure you."

The gate-guards' laughter was coarse and heavy. "You sound as though you know, Master Oswald!"

"Well, I've seen the damage she's left behind her. The woman has a sharp mind, Sergeant, and a sharp tongue to match it; be wary of her. I'll have no worry about trusting her to take my cloth out for trading, I assure you."

"A gentlewoman?" The soldier sounded outraged. "Alone?"

"Oh, I'll hire a bodyguard or two to go with her, and another gentlewoman to help her, never fear."

"Ho! Four, in place of yourself alone? What profit's in that, Master Oswald?"

"Quite a bit," Allouene said in her most musical tones. "I drive a hard bargain, soldier."

They whooped, and the sergeant bantered with her, a few gibes about the worth of her goods—but Magnus realized that the corporal was silent. They respected class barriers, indeed—only gentry could flirt with gentry.

Finally, the sergeant said, "Well, there's no reason to search your wagon, Master Oswald, and we've a serf with a cart coming up behind you. Be off with you now, and good trading to you!"

"Why, thank you, Sergeant, and a good day to you!"

The wagon began to move again, and all four hidden passengers let out a silent sigh of relief. Magnus began to realize just how solid a base Master Oswald had established here, if he was so well-known and trusted that the guards at the city gate would let him pass without the slightest search—and he realized from that, that Master Oswald had been taking something of a risk in calling for additional agents. What did he really know about them, after all? Only that if SCENT had accepted them, they must be trustworthy—and Magnus knew, from his own reservations, what kind of limits there might be to that.

The wagon turned corners twice. Then the rumble of the wheels changed timbre, from the grating of cobblestones to the hollow rumble of wood. They came to a stop; then the tarpaulin was pulled back, and they sat up, breathing deeply of the fresh air— well, relatively fresh; it was redolent of hay and horses and their by-products, but it was still a pleasant change.

"Out with you, and down." Oswald pointed to a dark stairway at the side of the stables.

They sighed, jumped down, and filed into the hole. Wooden steps led down six feet, to Allouene, who was lighting a lantern. Its light showed them a cellar, walled with fieldstone and floored with earth. Sections of tree trunk held up wooden beams seven feet overhead; Magnus almost had to stoop. Casks lined one wall, bottles another.

Oswald came down and saw the direction of their

gaze. He grinned. "I'm a draper, but I do a little tavern trade on the side, with a room or two to let out by the night. It's a convenient cover to have people coming and going."

"Going where?" Lancorn asked, but Oswald only shook his head. "Not out here. Come along." He led them through a timber door and into another room. Magnus noticed that the door was four inches thick, and solid. He looked up and saw a wooden ceiling. "Is that as thick as the door?"

Master Oswald nodded. "Four inches thick, with the beams closely fitted—and even if there were a gap or two from shrinkage, it wouldn't matter; that's only a pantry above us, and the cook and scullery maids don't linger long in it."

Footsteps sounded overhead, and they all fell silent, looking up—but the footsteps crossed the ceiling, then crossed back, and they heard a door closing.

Master Oswald looked back down at them, grinning. "See? This room is secure." He stepped around a large table that held a sheaf of papers, a large leather-bound book, and an abacus. "This is my tavern office, if we need an excuse." He pulled out a drawer and drew out a large roll of parchment. He unrolled it across the top of the desk, set paperweights on the corners, and they found themselves looking at a map of the continent. "Now," said Master Oswald, "I'd like the five of you to wander about the city—in pairs or threes, mind—just to get the feel of things, and make sure your dialect matches one of the ones you'll hear. Then, when you're feeling secure, I'll send each of you on a trading mission, so you can get the lay of the land and come up with ideas for tactics. But I'll tell you the broad strategy." He put a finger on the map, near the large blue amoeboid of the inland sea. "This is where we are— Orthoville, the capital city. The King's here, not that anyone ever sees much of him, and it's the natural place to spread ideas." He traced boundary lines with his fingers, and pointed to large dots. "These are the duchies, and the dukes' capitals. The roads run out as rays, from Orthoville to the dukes' seats."

"Convenient," Ragnar muttered.

Oswald nodded. "Everything is for the lords' convenience—and protection; those roads follow the high ground, and give the King a quick way to send a strike force to reinforce any lord who's having trouble—not that this particular king seems about to do much. So any ideas we can plant in a lord's retinue, will go right out to the country with him."

"Are there no roads that connect town to town?" Silfot asked.

"Yes, dirt roads, only wide enough for one cart at a time. But I see your meaning, friend, yes." Oswald nodded. "Your best bet is to go from village to village, singing for your supper. Let's get together on the lyrics, though, eh?"

Siflot smiled and ducked his head in answer. It was their first reminder that Oswald was in charge, and that whatever they were going to do, they were going to do it his way.

"So much for Propaganda of the Word," Oswald said. "We'll plant ideas, in conversation or in stories or, best of all, songs. People will repeat the message more often if we can hit upon a tune that catches on—and they'll repeat it with less distortion, because of the rhyme. In fact, I've worked out a few variations on popular songs already—if we change them as they circulate, we'll get across some basic ideas of human rights."

"I could redo Robin Hood so that his band voted on decisions," Siflot offered.

Master Oswald nodded. "Good idea, but not yet. Right now, just having Robin Hood at all, is enough. Same idea for Propaganda of the Deed—no terrorism, no bombings, just helping serfs escape and teaching them how to defend themselves in their hideouts. If we can build up a few bands of free men, word will spread, and other people will get the idea."

Magnus frowned. "But if they gain too much fame, the lords will send armies to wipe them out."

"Unfortunate, but probably unavoidable," Oswald agreed. "If they make a gallant last stand, though, it will fire the minds and hearts of serfs everywhere—if we make sure they hear about it."

Magnus stood immobile, telling himself that Master Oswald couldn't really have meant that to be as cold-blooded as it sounded.

"But if we can build up large enough bands," Ragnar objected, "couldn't they strike back at the lords?"

"I said, not yet." Oswald held up a hand. "We're not after a revolution here—that's standard SCENT policy. If we overthrew the lords right now, who would take their place? Just peasants who were rougher and tougher than average—and the first thing you know, you'd have the same system in place all over again, but with different masters. Only this time, they'd know what to watch out for, and they'd be even tougher to overthrow. No, we'll work the fundamental concepts of democracy into their culture first, then move toward a new system one change at a time. That way, when the lords are finally kicked out, they'll stay out, and government by the people will have a chance."

"All right," Lancorn said. "Technological determinism. We introduce a technological innovation—say, the printing press—and it will cause a change in the economy, which will cause a change in the social structure, making the middle class dominant. That will cause a change in the political structure, making them move toward parliamentary government—and that would change the value structure."

This time both Allouene and Oswald shook their heads, and Allouene said, "No major technological innovations—that's the cornerstone of SCENT policy. Bring in earthshaking inventions like that, and the social change will be an explosion, not normal growth. The society will tear itself apart trying to readjust, and thousands of people will be maimed and killed in the process. The English Civil War was a mild example—but 'mild' only because the technological innovations had been imported two hundred years before. Even with that much time, the society *still* couldn't adapt fast enough to avoid war."

"Besides," Oswald said, "technological innovations don't come just one at a time. The printing press wouldn't make much difference without the rise of a literate merchant class to read the books."

"And the middle class rose because of better ships and better navigation equipment, such as the astrolabe and the pendulum clock." Lancorn nodded, chagrined. "You can't take just one."

"Not even in a culture that doesn't know anything about modern technology," Master Oswald confirmed. "But here, the lords *do* know about the astrolabe, the compass, the pendulum clock, and the printing press—and they know about the English Civil War, too. Worse, they know about the French Revolution, when the social changes had been dammed up too long and broke loose in a flood. So they're very wary, very watchful—and at the slightest sign there was a printing press around, they'd track it down, break it to splinters, and kill the printer."

"I thought you were a merchant," Ragnar said, frowning. "Can't you justify new and improved transportation?"

"Such as the steam engine?" Oswald shook his head. "They'd be onto me in a minute. I do my trading by ox-cart and wagon. It's enough to keep a merchant prosperous, and keep the necessary minimum of trade going. But any sign of improvements, the lords would eliminate instantly—I've seen it happen. One merchant started building his own roads, going places the lords didn't want—and he disappeared in the middle of the night, was never heard from again. Another one started to set up an exchange network with other merchants—and they *all* disappeared. No, the aristocrats know what new inventions and new systems mean, and they make sure they don't happen."

"Well, won't they stop our songs?" Lancorn asked.

"They can't, even if they outlaw them—people will just sing them in secret, and that by itself will stimulate the spirit of defiance. But more importantly, you need to come up with stories and songs that the lords themselves will like, and that are such good fun, and seem so innocent, that any aristocrat who starts analyzing them for messages will be pooh-poohed by his fellows."

"How can we do that?" Lancorn asked.

"Try," Oswald suggested. "The Robin Hood ballads were just as popular in the medieval courts as they were in the peasant villages. Nobody wants to identify with the bad guy, after all. Technological determinism ends with a new political system developing a new value-system, and that means the pyramid can be worked in reverse—change the value system, and you can change the political structure."

Magnus shook his head. "They will not allow it. These lords are firmly entrenched, from what you say; only war will rid the serfs of their yoke. The lords have the monopoly on violence, after all."

"True," Oswald admitted, "but if we do the groundwork well enough, we can keep it down to a series of skirmishes. We have to prepare for that outbreak, or you'll have nothing but an abortive rebellion with an awful lot of dead peasants, and nothing but worse oppression for the survivors."

They were all quiet, looking at one another, recognizing the truth in Oswald's words.

"For now, breakfast." Oswald rolled up the map. "Then you can start roaming the city—and looking for weak spots in the social wall."

The day passed quickly, in a dizzying kaleidoscope of dialects and locations—markets, workshops, churches, prison. Before long, Siflot was juggling in front of an audience, then demonstrating his expertise as an acrobat, which none of his team had known about. He brought home quite a haul in copper coins, too.

The others didn't trust themselves to say much, especially Magnus, who stood tall enough to stand out horribly, and drew suspicious looks from guardsmen all around town. He was challenged on more than one occasion, but the guards seemed satisfied with his explanation that he was a new bodyguard from a small village, hired by Master Oswald to protect his shipments of cloth.

It made Magnus realize how strong the police presence was.

Ragnar found out, too, by pretending to get drunk and picking a few fights. The guardsmen were there very quickly, though they just stood and watched.

"Three fights, and not a single criminal contacted me," he told the rest of them that night, in disgust. "Don't they have any crime here?"

"Only as much as the aristocrats want," Oswald assured him. "The vices flourish, because the lords like to take advantage of them now and then—but theft and violence are squashed at the first sign; they don't want to take any chances that serfs

159

might learn to fight back. They don't *waste* criminals, of course—they just send them to the mines, or the galleys."

Magnus shuddered; there was something inhuman in back of it all.

The days passed quickly, and before he knew it, he and Ragnar were out riding guard for a pair of wagons driven by husky serfs, with Lancorn and Allouene to take care of the goods and do the buying and selling. Siflot disappeared about the same time, to go wandering from village to village and eventually castle to castle, singing songs, doing gymnastics, carrying news—and spreading hints that serfs were fully human, not a subspecies. He surfaced every few weeks, either at Master Oswald's, or just "coincidentally" showing up in the same village the others were staying in for the night—at which time, they exchanged news of a different order from Siflot's stock in trade.

"I always wanted to be a journalist," he confided to Magnus one evening.

Magnus, however, had not always wanted to be a bodyguard. Two trips riding shotgun for Lancorn and Allouene, and Master Oswald officially discharged him from his service, sending him out to look for employment on his own. Magnus found that his size made him very desirable to other merchants, and even for one lord who wanted a larger-than-usual troop to march around his estates for a week, to overawe his serfs. Magnus was glad there was no offer of permanent employment; he wasn't anxious to be tied down to one lord just yet.

There actually was a battle; two lords had a boundary dispute, and let the serfs fight it out for them. Magnus found himself in the position of temporary lieutenant, trying to train and command a bunch of plowboys. He devoted himself to trying to get as many of them as possible through the skirmish alive. His tactics worked in more ways than one—he lost only two, and his side won; a quick victory was the easiest way to save lives. The other officers were suspicious of him, knowing he'd had a great deal more to do with the victory than he should have, but unable to say why—so they were very glad when the lord discharged him and sent him on his way.

So was Magnus; the oppression of the serfs was beginning to sicken him, and seeing men toss away their lives just to settle a lord's argument was the worst yet.

In between, as he rode the dusty roads looking for work, he studied the other travellers he saw— clerics and merchants, couriers and farmers with carts, lords with their entourages, vagabonds and, yes, madmen—or, at least, very simple-minded beggars. No one gave them much money, but no one paid them much attention, either—and Magnus began to realize that he had another cover available, if ever he needed one.

All through it, he waited impatiently for an escaped serf to rescue, or even to hear of one –but there was never a word. Apparently, no matter how oppressed they were, the serfs knew better than to try to flee.

Finally, though, a troop of soldiers stepped out

from a tree and stopped him with raised pikes. Magnus stopped, but did not raise his hands, only frowning down at the men.

"State your name and business!" the sergeant barked.

"Gar Pike, and I am a mercenary looking for work." Magnus took him in at a glance. "From the look of you, I'd say you could use my services."

"We'll do well enough without any strangers!" the sergeant barked. "You know the law—say if you've seen a serf boy fleeing."

Inside, Magnus's heart sang, but he didn't let it show in his face. "Not a trace."

"If you do, Milord Murthren will pay you five pounds of silver for him," the sergeant growled. "Three pounds, if he's dead."

Magnus gave him a wolfish smile. "I'll see what I can find." Two more pounds, alive! What information did the boy have that the lord wanted?

"Watch carefully," the sergeant warned. "He's only ten, and not yet branded."

That by itself was something of a shock. Magnus had never yet seen a serf without the telltale brand on the back of one hand—a gothic letter S, for "serf." He hadn't known there was an age limit.

He nodded, and assured the sergeant, "I'll bring in anything I can find." But he didn't say to what destination he would bring the boy.

He hunted, and eavesdropped telepathically—so, although he hadn't heard the Safety Base's radio beacon himself, he read Lord Murthren's thoughts and learned of it. It was going to be a race, he knew—to see if he could get there before the soldiers did.

But he had, and Ian was hiking by his side now, safe unless Lord Murthren could recognize every single one of his serfs. All in all, Magnus felt fairly secure.

CHAPTER
~8~

The house seemed magnificent to Ian. It was two stories high with a gable above the second story, and half-timbered—the walls outside were very rough plaster, with the great wooden beams of the house-frame showing clearly. The windows were divided into twelve little squares, each filled with glass, real glass, and the door had a metal lock as well as a bar-latch. The shop was open, though it was barely past sunrise, so Gar and Ian went right in, and stepped into a heady scent of dye and cloth.

Inside, the house was divided into two rooms. The front was huge, as wide as the house, and square. It was filled with tables, upon which were piled bolts of cloth in all manner of colors and textures. There were velvets, satins, even silks, as well as common broadcloth and monk's cloth. Gar's friend was a draper, a cloth-merchant.

The back room, in which they met the merchant

165

Oswald, was much smaller, only twelve feet deep and half the width of the house. It was still quite large to Ian's eyes, and was Master Oswald's office. He had a great wooden table for a desk with a counting-frame propped up at an angle, and his most precious bolts of cloth locked in great wooden chests with huge iron padlocks. Master Oswald looked up, surprised, when Gar walked in. Then he saw Ian, coming in behind Gar, and stared, astonished—and, yes, alarmed. He recovered quickly, though, and stood up, arms open in greeting and smiling. "So, you are back so soon, Gar!"

"It was this young fellow who speeded me, Oswald." Gar clapped Ian's shoulder. "Meet my new apprentice. His name is Ian Tobinson, and he has agreed to bear my shield, should I have one, and to cook my meals and pitch my tent."

Ian looked about him, wondering. He had hoped for a home for a little while—but he had scarcely imagined something so grand as this!

"Well, well!" Master Oswald's gaze swiveled to the boy. "And young enough to have no brand, I see! We shall have to dress him as befits his station." He frowned. "You've apprenticed yourself to a hard trade, my boy."

Ian felt obliged to say something. He thought quickly and forced out the words: "I am thankful to Master Gar for taking me, sir."

Oswald smiled, amused, and nodded. "So you should be, my boy. Days of strife are coming for this land. It will be well for a man to know how to use a sword, and you could have no better teacher than Captain Pike."

Ian looked up at Gar, astonished. He hadn't known the free-lance was a captain!

Oswald cocked an eyebrow at Gar. "Have you fed?"

"Not for hours," Gar said, grinning.

"Well enough, my lad," Oswald chuckled, "though you've called me an old mother hen often enough." He thrust back his sleeves. "Naetheless, I think we can fill that belly of yours, even if 'tis with naught but porridge. Come along."

He led them down a short flight of stairs, and Ian found himself marveling. This was the second time in his life he had seen such a staircase, the first having been in the Stone Egg. What a fine thing it was to be a gentleman!

They came down into a hall walled with rough plaster. Oswald turned to his right and led them through a narrow door into a kitchen. A lean woman with a sharp chin leaned over a pot, eyes narrowed against the smoke.

"Two more for breakfast, Matilda!" Oswald called.

"We would be grateful for the porridge, Matilda," Gar said. "I have journeyed all night on your master's business, and the least he owes me is a hearty meal."

The old cook gave him a gap-toothed smile, which seemed surprising in so severe a face. "Eh, seat yourself, Master Gar. I'll have your porridge shortly—another pot for me master." She squinted, peering at Ian. "And who is this?"

"My new apprentice," Gar said easily. "His old master thought him too quarrelsome to be a weaver."

Matilda frowned. "A blank-shield soldier, taking an apprentice?" She hobbled over to Ian and bent down to peer into his face. Then she grinned again and turned back to her stove, cackling and shaking her head. "Aye, he's naught but your apprentice, Master Gar! Aye, surely!"

"How now, you old hag!" Gar's voice was still good-natured. "He is my apprentice, nothing more and nothing less, I say!"

"Aye, aye." Matilda nodded, stirring her porridge. "Your 'prentice and nothing more, I'll be bound, and no reason to take him save to aid a poor weaver who had a ruffian on his hands! Oh, aye, Master Gar! And there is none of your blood in him, as these old eyes can see!"

"Well . . ." Gar contrived to look embarrassed, and cleared his throat. "You have caught me fairly, Matilda. He is, my, uh, nephew."

"Oh, aye." Matilda looked up at him wide-eyed, then nodded wisely. "Bless thee, Master Gar. Oh, how you could have fooled me."

Ian looked up at Gar in surprise. Could there really be any resemblance between himself and the swordsman?

Then he realized that the cook was old, near-sighted, and probably half-blind, and the resemblance was probably more in her mind than in his face.

Gar squeezed his shoulder, and Ian looked up to

see the free-lance wink and smile. He grinned back. If the cook believed the story Gar had intended to tell anyway, so much the better.

"Seat yourselves," Matilda called, tilting the pot and scraping out two huge bowlfuls of porridge. "Sit and eat your breakfast, before it sets."

They ate in a room just for dining, with Master Oswald—and they ate hugely, with milk and honey on their porridge. Ian could scarcely believe his eyes, or his mouth—milk and honey were for the lords, and thick porridge was only for the gentry! His own breakfast, as long as he could remember, had been only thin gruel.

He ate his fill and a little more, until the bowl was empty; then he sat back with a great sigh and a very full stomach.

Gar looked up and smiled. "Had enough, lad?"

Ian nodded and blinked. Suddenly, he felt very sleepy. He yawned hugely, and Gar chuckled. "Aye, I'm beginning to feel the night's strains a bit myself." He turned to the cook. "Where shall my nephew doss down?"

"In the attic, good soldier," the cook answered. "He can fall asleep on a pile of straw, like any other young 'prentice." She hobbled over to Ian and scooped him out of the chair, more by gesture than by strength, and ushered him out into the kitchen.

Once there, though, she paused, pursing her lips. "Nay, I think not—the other 'prentices will be just waking as you'd be lying down. Bad for them, that— give them ideas of laziness, it would. Besides, you'll need long sleep, after being on the road all night,

with Master Gar." She glanced down at Ian. "You did
ride by night, didn't you?"

Ian wasn't sure whether or not he should tell her,
then realized he couldn't dissemble much if he were
going to sleep during the day. "Aye, mum."

"So I thought." Matilda thrust her lower lip out
and sucked on her few remaining teeth, considering.
"We'll put you in the pantry for the day. Let me see,
now—what stores will I need? A sack of potatoes, another of flour, and two measures of dried pease." She
nodded, satisfied, and pushed him toward the door at
the back of the kitchen. "Bring me those, then settle
yourself!"

Ian made two trips of it, reflecting that this fetch-
ing and carrying didn't guarantee him a sound sleep.
Matilda was bound to think of something she'd for-
gotten, and come bustling in to fetch it, or to send
her scullery maid, if she had one—and she might
make a second trip, or a third. Ian determined that he
would sleep soundly no matter how much noise she
made. He brought the sack of flour last, and could
just barely manage it—it was very heavy. Matilda
blinked at him, surprised. "Well, then, manikin!
Master Gar may make a soldier of you yet!"

But Ian scarcely heard her; he had already turned
away to the pantry, nodding. He threw himself down
on three huge bags of flour, and was instantly asleep.

Ian was awakened by a loud clatter of dishes and
Matilda scolding at her scullery maid. He sat bolt upright, startled by the noise, then realized what it was,
smiled, and lay down. The sun was coming in the

eastern window; he could only have slept a few hours. He closed his eyes and settled himself for sleep again. . . .

"But how did the boy find the entrance to one of the Safety Bases?"

Ian opened his eyes, surprised. He frowned and looked over the side of his improvised bed. There was a crack between the floorboards; through it, he could see Master Oswald's bald head. Was there a secret room beneath him? No, surely not, he chided himself—only a very ordinary, and un-secret, cellar. Surely. He heard Gar's voice rise in answer to the draper: "It must have been an accident. He certainly could not have reasoned out how to open the hatch."

Ian squirmed. It wasn't right to eavesdrop. He was sorely tempted, but he resolved to be good. He forced himself to turn over, face away from the crack in the floor, and closed his eyes tight, willing himself to sleep.

However, he might have been willing, but sleep was not, and he couldn't shut out the voices—nor could he come out into the kitchen after so short a while. What would he say if Matilda asked him what he was doing up and about when he'd been told to sleep? That he was turning away from the voices? When he wasn't even supposed to know about them?

"How could they have known he was there?" It was Master Oswald's voice. "They must have, for they came to bring him back."

"He must have activated the beacon by accident," Gar answered. "Certainly a boy from this culture would never have figured out a control panel by himself. Serfs can't even read."

"True," Master Oswald rumbled. "Even the free-lance who hid there with me couldn't figure it out, and he was a gentleman, who had had some education, or what passes for it in a medieval culture. But how do you know this boy isn't a spy from the lords, who *does* know how to operate such controls?"

Ian stiffened. Could Master Oswald really think such of him? But no—Captain Gar's voice indicated that by its tone, as he answered. "Possible, of course—but unlikely, since he's a child. And if he were, why would he have come out before his help arrived?"

"Perhaps he knew it was close."

Ian could hear the smile in Gar's voice. "If his help had arrived, why would he have run away with me? No, I'm almost certain he's a local boy."

"*Almost* certain." Master Oswald pounced on it. "You're not really sure, then."

"Quite sure." Gar was still amused.

"But just in case, we have him where we can watch him."

So that was why Gar had helped him! A knot twisted itself up in Ian's belly. Had the free-lance aided him only because he did not trust him?

"Besides," Gar went on, "I like the boy."

The knot loosened, a little.

"You've taken a liking to him awfully quickly." Master Oswald growled.

"Amazingly so," Gar agreed. "Any kid who's willing to brave the dangers of that forest, and take on a two-hundred-mile walk at his age, just because he wants to be free . . . well, I'm on his side."

"So am I," Master Oswald admitted. "But encumbering yourself with a child could be very foolish. I needn't remind you how much of a liability he could be, to someone who has to stay on the move—and secretly!"

"Or how much of an asset," Gar countered. "He knows things about this culture I could only guess at—and I'd trust him a lot further than any adult."

The knot loosened the rest of the way, and Ian resolved that he would prove Captain Pike right to have trusted him.

"Yes," Master Oswald mused. "That brings us to why he ran away from home. As to that, I had some news last night, after you had gone. It seems one of Lord Murthren's serfs had helped his daughter to escape into the forest—just in time, too, because Lord Murthren had noticed her, all too favorably."

Gar whistled. "The lord himself? The poor lass was in for trouble!"

"A lot," Master Oswald agreed, "a great deal of trouble. Her father helped her escape, and they whipped him within an inch of his life for it."

Ian squeezed his eyes shut and clenched his jaw, fighting to keep from crying out, trying to banish the sight of his father lashed to the post.

"Brave man," Gar whispered.

"Very," Master Oswald agreed. "He went on to urge his son to run away—when he'd just been taken down from the whipping-post and needed somebody to care for him, he told his son to run away right then, when they'd least expect it. The kid ran—a boy too young to have a brand."

"And they flogged the father again?" Gar asked.

"No, he cheated them. He died first, before they discovered the boy was missing."

The cellar was very quiet. Ian felt the ache within him expand, hollowing him out; two hot tears forced their way through his clenching eyelids.

"So." Gar's voice was soft. "Our young guest really needs a friend."

"He's a brave boy," Oswald admitted, "and an orphan now—the mother had died a while before."

"You had the news quickly," Gar said, in tones of respect, "and thoroughly."

"That's my job," Oswald growled.

"Well, I have some information for you, too," Gar said, "something we very narrowly managed to avoid on the way back here."

"A troop of soldiers, of course."

"More than that—Lord Murthren himself."

"Lord Murthren!" Master Oswald sounded amazed—and, yes, alarmed. "Out hunting a simple serf boy by himself?"

"No, he had a troop with him," Gar said grimly, "but yes, he was definitely leading them in person. He said something about the boy having violated one of the Secret Places of the Old Ones."

It was very quiet in the room below. Ian lay very still, and tried not to breathe.

"He couldn't have known that when the boy escaped," Master Oswald said.

"No," Gar said. "So . . ."

A WIZARD IN ABSENTIA

"So he received the distress beacon, too," Master Oswald snapped, "which means he has a scanner."

"And knows how to operate it," Gar pointed out.

"Yes." Master Oswald's voice had hardened, but began to sound sarcastic now, too. "And, although Lord Murthren is one of the two or three top aristocrats in the land, he's hacked his way to that position on his own. His father was only a count."

"Of course," Gar said, "it's possible that the King gave him a scanner, and taught him how to use it *after* he'd become a top counsellor. However . . ."

"However." Master Oswald sounded as though he were grinning like a cat, licking cream from his whiskers. "However, he probably inherited the rig from his father, who inherited it from *his* father— and on and on back."

"Chances are that it's probably been there since the colonizing ship landed," Gar put in.

"Exactly," Master Oswald grumbled. "And if even a petty count in the backwoods has a scanner and knows how to use it . . ."

"Probably," Gar finished, "*all* the lords do."

"So that's one more piece of technological knowledge they've kept," Oswald said, with an air of satisfaction. "Possibly ritualized—you know, you push this button, and then that button, and twist this dial, and the thing does what it's supposed to do, and they do it as part of their daily duties. . . ."

"The same way that they know how to operate their machine guns and pocket nuclear bombs," Gar agreed, "and how to make more ammunition. And

175

they're lucky their ancestors made the blasted things damn near indestructible."

"They know how to clean them and maintain them, presumably," Oswald said, "but again, only as a ritual. 'You must do this and this and this to your machine gun when you waken every morning, or it will fail you when you need it.' That's how they know how to make gunpowder, too—just follow the recipe, pour the powder into the casing, and squeeze the bullet in on top."

"Making brass casings is a strain on a Baroque metalsmith, I'll agree, but it's possible, especially with hand-me-down equipment from a high-tech culture," Gar said, "once he's been shown how. He wouldn't understand what he was doing or why, but he could do it."

"Rimfire," Master Oswald said. "Who couldn't? And that's why the ancestors went to slug-throwers instead of beamers, of course—something just barely within the capabilities of a Baroque society. That's probably the way they use their safety bases—by rote."

"Self-repairing," Gar said, "not that they'd need anything beyond cleaning, hardly any maintenance. Last forever."

"As they have," Master Oswald agreed, "or for five hundred years, at least."

They were silent a moment. Then Master Oswald said suddenly, "Where's the boy heading, anyway?"

"Castlerock," Gar said. "So he says, anyway."

"Castlerock!" Master Oswald was delighted. "No!

You mean it? That far in the backwoods, and he's heard of Castlerock?"

"Heard enough about it to want to go there," Gar confirmed. "After all, it's the only place an escaped serf can go and be even halfway safe."

"So even here, they've heard there's an island off the north coast that serfs have been escaping to for the last dozen years! That campaign is taking very firm hold."

"Word gets around," Gar said, "especially among an oppressed population. When virtual slaves hear of an island in the Central Sea where serfs can actually hold off their masters' armies, it captures the imagination."

"Hope," Master Oswald agreed. "Even if they can't escape, they can hope—for themselves, but even more for their children."

"Which plants the seed of unrest," Gar noted, "and which is why the masters have to stamp it out, as quickly as they can."

"They may have better capabilities than we've seen so far," Master Oswald growled. "If they have scanners, they may have blast-cannon, and fliers. Besides, there's that slender, very well-contained off-planet trade. What's to stop them from hiring a merchant captain to land on Castlerock, and burn everyone to cinders with his exhaust?"

"Nothing but his conscience," Gar said grimly. "Are our men working on the captains?"

"We're making some progress there . . ." And Master Oswald was off into a sea of terms that Ian didn't understand, words like "capital" and "interest" and "extension of terms."

Actually, there had been so many of those that he had only barely been able to grasp the gist of what they had said. What was a "scanner," he wondered, and a "distress beacon" and a "machine gun"? He grasped the general idea, though: when he had accidentally pressed that circle on the table in the Stone Egg, it had somehow sent out a message that had called in Lord Murthren. Fortunately, though, Gar seemed to have heard it, too, and had come and saved him.

The nobles had magical things—everyone knew that . . .

Except, perhaps, Gar and Master Oswald? They had been talking as though these magical talismans were news to them, as though they had just discovered something that they had only suspected before. And, since everyone in the kingdom knew about the talismans, these two men must be from a foreign country.

Spies!

Ian's blood chilled, sending a shiver through him. He lay there wondering, dread pooling in him. . . .

Then he remembered—they had spoken of Castlerock, spoken of it as though they had something to do with it. They were helping Castlerock, then! Helping serfs, like himself! They were on his side, to protect him against the lords, against Lord Murthren. He relaxed again, smiling—his judgement of Gar had been right—the man was good . . .

And Castlerock was real.

Ian closed his eyes and drifted off to sleep in spite of the murmuring voices from beneath the floor. He would go to Castlerock, and be free!

Ian woke after sunset. He came out of the pantry, yawning and rubbing his eyes. Matilda peered at him. "Eh! It's you, is it? Slept well enough, did you?" She pointed a finger at a chair by the wall. "There be your new clothes. Into them quickly, and don't be long about it, for your new master . . ." (and for some reason Ian could not understand, she giggled at this) ". . . your new master has a wish to be up and away right soon. You're to be setting out for the north tonight, the both of you."

The north! Ian's heart leaped. Yes, he would certainly be dressed quickly!

He turned toward the chair to pick up the clothing, then stood still, frozen in amazement. "But—these cannot be for me!" There on the chair were not a serf's rough tunic and leggins and cross-gartered sandals, but a jerkin and hose, such as a gentleman's son might wear, though they were made out of plain broadcloth—a green jerkin and brown hose, and real leather boots! And hanging over the back of the chair was a sword, a real sword—boy-sized, but real for all that!

Matilda gave him a gap-toothed grin. "Aye, they're for you, manikin. Not what you're used to, I'll wager. But your new master is a man of means, and you'll have to get used to it." She brandished her big wooden ladle in a mock threat. "Get along with you, now, for there's no time to waste!"

Ian gathered up the clothes and ducked back into the pantry. He came out a few minutes later, feeling like a prince in his finery.

"Sit ye down, now," Matilda said, jabbing her spoon at the table. "Don't bother about what you're eating, and be quick about it, for you must travel long and far tonight, and you can't manage it on too full a stomach."

Ian stared at the plate of beef for a moment. Then he shook himself and sat down at the table. He wondered if he would get used to having meat so often.

He was just finishing when Gar came in, with Master Oswald behind him. He grinned at Ian. "Well, then! Finished, are you?" He sat down at the other side of the table. "Still, take your time. We've quite a bit to tell you before we set out for the north. We must look as though we're only going for a short stroll in the moonlight."

Ian swallowed and stood up. "I'm ready now, sir."

"I'm not." Gar tapped the table with a forefinger. "I've much to tell you, as I said. Matilda! Some tea, if you have it!"

"If I have it?" The old cook snorted in indignation. "When was the day that there wasn't a simmering kettle on the stove in this house, and a pot of tea ready to brew! If I have it, indeed!" And in very short order, there were mugs of tea before each of them. There was a third cup at the side of the table where Master Oswald was just sitting down. "Now, then, Matilda!" he chuckled. "I do imagine the captain had no idea."

"Live like animals, that's what," Matilda snorted.

"Now don't bother me, silly menfolk! We've dishes to wash and pots to scour, and a kitchen to get in order."

Ian sipped at his hot, strong tea, marvelling at its flavor while Gar explained their journey. "A lord in the north has need of troops, Ian, for he is beset by his rival noblemen. They haven't marched on him yet, but they will soon, or I mistake the news completely."

"He is a most worthy lord," Master Oswald rumbled. "He treats his serfs well. They say that when one of them dies, he weeps as though at the death of a kinsman."

Or a favorite dog, Ian thought—but he didn't say so.

"They die mostly of old age, or disease," Gar put in.

"Only diseases that can't be cured," Master Oswald said, nodding. "He keeps three doctors on his estates, besides his own personal physician. If one of his serfs falls sick, he—or his lady, while she lived—goes out to look after that one, themselves."

"So they die on his estates only rarely," Gar said. "You may have heard of him—Lord Aran."

He caught Ian with tea in his mouth; he swallowed convulsively, and almost choked on it. He coughed; Master Oswald leaned over and thumped him on the back, grinning. "Ah, yes—I'd say you've heard of him, lad."

Ian looked up, wiping his streaming eyes, and nodded. He had heard tales of Count Aran's estates—was there a serf in his village who hadn't? They said he treated his serfs as though they were free men, with respect and honor. "They say," he said, "that serfs are whipped on his estates only rarely—and then only for harsh offenses, such as striking another man who is weaker than he, or stealing."

"But stealing from another serf." Master Oswald nodded. "He doubles the number of strokes if they steal from a gentleman, and triples it for a nobleman—but the punishment is the same. It is the crime he punishes, not its object."

"But even so, they are never flogged more than forty lashes," Gar said. "Ten for a serf, twenty for a gentleman or a serf woman, thirty for a nobleman or a gentlewoman, forty for a noblewoman. That is his code. Beyond that, it is death for murder or rape."

Master Oswald nodded. "His justice is famous. He treats his serfs as men, not as animals who are his property."

"He is a man I could fight for with a good conscience." Gar winked at Oswald and sipped from his cup.

Ian wondered about the wink.

Master Oswald said, with sarcasm, "Good conscience—and I understand he pays well, too."

"Aye, that is one thing about good treatment of serfs." Gar leaned forward, suddenly serious. "His land produces much more than that of his neighbors."

Master Oswald spread his hands. "What can you expect? He gives each serf a plot of land and says, 'This is your own, for as long as I am lord here. You must give me half of your harvest, but the rest is yours to do with as you will. Keep it, or sell it—and if you sell it, the money is yours.' Will not the serfs, then, labor harder on the land, to produce more?"

Gar nodded. "Yet they are still there to labor together on one another's fields, and on his. Of course they produce more—and his neighbor lords are jealous."

"Certainly, certainly! No man likes to see his equal get ahead of him. But will they follow his methods, and mimic his ways of dealing with his serfs, so that they may produce more on their own land?"

"No, of course not. They will band together to tell him he must cease to treat his serfs so well."

"You cannot blame them." Master Oswald grinned. "If his ways caught on, their serfs might begin to think they have rights as human beings, too— that they are humans, not animals. They might even begin to show some evidence of self-respect. Thus does he breed discontent."

Ian followed the conversation, looking from man to man, wide-eyed. "Rights?" What were those?

"Yes, the rights of men," Gar agreed, "and what happens then, to the privileges and the tyranny of the lords?"

A whole new world was opening within Ian's mind. That serfs might consider themselves men— poor and uncultured, but just as good inside as gentlemen, or even lords! Even more, though—that the power of the lords was not absolute, that it could be resisted, perhaps even lessened! He almost gasped out loud—it was an amazing thought, and the possibilities it opened were limitless! Whole companies of serfs might go to places like Castlerock, or bury themselves in the fastnesses of the forest, and farm for themselves, and be free in their own right, be their own lords! As far as he could tell, Count Aran ruled his people, but did not oppress them—his serfs did not think to disobey, but they dared to stand in his presence, and even disagree with him! What could they do, he wondered, if Count Aran became like all the others, like Lord Murthren? Would his serfs submit, as his fellows had? Or would they oust Count Aran, and choose another lord?

His brain reeled, and he shut off the speculations; they were too confusing, he could not deal with them. What manner of men were Master Oswald and Master Gar, that they could speak of such things so casually and with no sign of fear? That one fragment of conversation he had overheard last night, still lingered in his mind. Castlerock . . .

"Enough of talk." Gar rose to his feet, clapping a hand to the sword hilt at his hip. "I must be off to action. I would see this paragon of governance with my own eyes, and how he manages his estates. Rumor is interesting, but it also has a way of being only half-true."

"Still," Master Oswald demurred, "there is always a grain of truth at the bottom of it."

Gar smiled sourly. "Not always. I have known men to start campaigns with rumors, Master Oswald. If they could discredit the leaders they hated, their men would fight with less verve." He grinned. "Thus have I come to have a taste for seeing

with my own eyes." He cocked an eyebrow at the
boy. "Haven't you, Ian?"

"Aye, most assuredly," Ian gasped, pulling himself
together and jumping to his feet. "Whenever you go,
Master Gar, I will ride wherever you wish!"

Gar's face twisted into a sardonic smile, and Ian's
heart stopped for a moment, afraid that he had of-
fended his protector. But Gar looked at Master
Oswald and said, "How quick to obey. My wish is his
law."

"It is not good," Master Oswald agreed heavily,
"but I do not doubt that, under your tutelage, he will
develop some belief in himself, Gar Pike. You will
make a man of him."

"I will indeed." Gar eyed Ian, measuring him. "He
will have the strength of the serfs when he's grown,
but will combine it with the hardness and toughness
of a warrior—and from such iron, we can forge a stalwart blade." He came around the table, clapping Ian
on the back. "Come, lad! Horse and hattock! Ho, and
away!"

Ten minutes later they were mounted, Gar on a
tall roan stallion and Ian, still not quite believing it
was happening, on a pony.

"Stay well, Oswald," Gar said, raising a hand in
farewell to his friend. "May the world prosper for
you."

"*Make* it prosper, Gar," Master Oswald returned.
"There's little enough I can do here, with my buying
and selling; it is you who must go out into the field
and make the great things happen."

Gar answered with a flat laugh. "I have more

knowledge than to believe that, Oswald," he said. "I don't underestimate my own part, mind you—I can visit the noblemen in their courts, and give things a shake here and there around the country. But you are the one who sees the points of weakness and sends us out to make the changes happen, whether I will it or not."

"Oh, I can find the right place to push," Master Oswald growled, "but those tremors might yield a harvest of bloodshed and suffering. It is you and your kind who will keep the cost down." His voice grew wistful. "Good luck to you—and farewell."

Gar waved in return, knocked his heels into his horse's sides, and rode off at a trot. The pony lurched into motion, and Ian hung on in a panic, barely managing to keep his seat. Gar looked back, grinning, then stared in surprise, and stopped his own mount. "I see," he said. "You haven't ridden before. Well, hold the reins above the saddlebow, lad, and keep to a walk until you get the knack of it."

Gar started up again, his horse at a walk. "And, Ian—slap his back with your reins." Ian did, and the pony began to walk forward after Gar's great roan.

So, walking their mounts, they passed out of Master Oswald's stableyard, and set off on their journey to Lord Aran's castle.

CHAPTER
~9~

They moved through the town without talking, Gar humming softly. It wasn't a long ride; houses and shops lined the street for only a hundred yards. They rode out past its limits and up a grade to the road. Gar turned right, to the north. Ian turned as well— but his mount did not.

Gar heard him calling to the pony, and looked back with a grin. "Pull on the right rein, and he'll turn."

Ian pulled, but too hard; the pony tossed his head, neighing in protest. "Gently, gently," Gar cautioned. "The bit rubs against the soft corners of his mouth. He'll answer to a gentle tug, mind you."

"I'm sorry." Ian stroked the pony's neck, hoping it wasn't angry with him.

"We're going to trot now," Gar said. "There's a trick to it—when the pony trots, he'll move up and down a great deal, and you don't want to be going down as he's going up, or you'll meet in the middle

with a smack that will jar your spine all the way up
to your skull. You must rise in your stirrups as he
goes up, then let yourself back into the saddle as
he goes down. So set your feet well, lad—that's what
the high heels on your boots are for. Put your weight
on them—have no fear, the straps won't break. Stand
in your stirrups halfway as his back comes up, sit
down as his back goes down, and you'll have a com-
fortable ride. Enough talking—are you ready?"

Ian swallowed. "Aye, sir."

"Try it, then." Gar knocked his heels gently into
his horse's sides, and the roan began to trot. Ian took
a deep breath, braced himself, kicked with his heels
tentatively—and the pony began to trot! He remembered what Gar had said and rose in his stirrups, but
not fast enough, and the saddle spanked him
soundly; then, as he was letting himself down, he
was too fast, and the saddle kicked him up again. He
pushed up and down frantically, but the saddle kept
spanking him. He almost thought the pony was getting even for that tug on the mouth.

"Try for the rhythm, lad!" Gar called out. "Like a
country dance!"

Ian tried.

It took a while, but he finally caught the knack of
it, with Gar calling encouragement. Ian began to actually enjoy it—but his legs began to ache, and he decided that there was more to riding than there looked
to be.

Gar took mercy on him and slowed his horse to a
walk. "Pull back on the reins, and he'll slow—but re-

member the tenderness of his mouth, and be gentle!"

Ian did as Gar bade him, and the pony slowed to a walk. Gar nodded in approval. "You catch it quickly, lad."

Quickly! Ian's bottom was already so sore that he wondered if he'd be able to walk when he dismounted—and he wasn't at all sure he'd ever want to ride again. But, "You'll be a decent horseman, by the time we reach Lord Aran's castle," Gar assured him. "It will take a year or more for you to learn it fully, though, even if you are a quick study."

"So long, sir?" Ian bleated in dismay.

"Oh, you'll be able to ride by the time we reach the castle," Gar said, lounging in his saddle. "That's two nights' ride. You take to the saddle so well, lad, that it will be like walking for you—or running. But to begin to think like a part of the horse? No, that takes time." He grinned down at Ian. "Don't let it bother you, lad. You've much else to learn, betimes. There're the dagger and the sword, for instance, and you must learn three different styles: saber, rapier, and straight sword. Then there's archery, as soon as we get you a bow. Never touched one, I gather?"

"Never." Ian shook his head. "Such things are only for serfs who are appointed soldiers by their lords—and for gentlemen like yourself."

"Of course." Gar nodded. "Serfs are allowed no weapons at all. I have seen it."

Ian wondered at the last phrase. Had the free-lance not grown up knowing that serfs were forbidden weapons? Again, he wondered: what manner of man *was* Gar?

"Then, too, you must learn to play the harp," Gar said, turning back to look at the road ahead. "A song may take you places where swordplay cannot. War does not always stride through this land; a mercenary should be able to turn his hand to a peaceful occupation, as well as a warlike one."

" 'Mercenary'?" Ian looked up. "What is that, sir?"

"Why, bless you, boy, that is you!" Gar grinned. "You and myself! A mercenary is a free-lance—a soldier who fights for money, rather than for friendship, or loyalty, or land. A mercenary is a soldier like me, Ian."

"Then that is what I wish to be." Ian nodded, sure that this much, at least, he would remember forever. "I shall learn quickly and well, sir!"

"I am certain of it." Gar leaned down to clap him on the shoulder. "But you must become a gentleman, Ian, and it will help if you know something of it, and therefore must I question you. To begin with, know you nothing of fighting?"

"With my fists, a little," Ian answered. "We boys were always fighting amongst ourselves in the village, though the men were not allowed to—and wrestling, of course."

Gar nodded. "Better than nothing, certainly. And, of course, the quarterstaff?"

"Oh, yes," Ian said. "The bailiff and soldiers encouraged us to learn that. Lord Murthren said that it was so that he could call us to fight for him as soldiers, if he needed us."

Gar frowned. "Strange."

Ian looked up. "Why, sir?"

Gar was slow in answering. "I should think your lord would not let you learn any skills that would allow you to fight against his soldiers, if it came into your head to do so."

"But it would not," Ian said, surprised. "What quarterstaff could hold against a sword, or even a halberd, my lord?'

"Any," Gar said flatly, and the answer jolted Ian. "If they never tell you that, though, you would never think of it. But there is a way a quarterstaff can best a sword—and be sure I'll teach you that. And, if you know a quarterstaff, you can learn a blade easily— well, not easily," he amended, "but you'll catch the knack of it more quickly."

"But Master Gar, it is against the law for a serf to touch weapons! If I am caught, they will hang me!"

Gar smiled, amused. "You are already a fugitive, lad. If they catch you, they'll flog you within an inch of your life, then make you walk home, and you'll probably die on the way. Which way would you rather pass?"

Ian swallowed, and was silent.

The free-lance was as good as his word; by the time they reached the castle of Lord Aran two days later, Ian had already learned how to care for the horses, saddle and bridle his own mount, pluck a few chords on the harp, and thrust and parry with his sword. Of course, Gar would not let him use the real blade, when the two of them dueled in practice, nor would he himself—he insisted they use willow wands. Then, after the practice, he demanded that Ian stand still, holding his sword across his palms at arm's length for a minute, then two, then three, then four, then five . . . Ian was amazed at how quickly his arms began to ache, but found he could bear it.

They chatted as they rode, Gar telling Ian amusing stories of his travels, and exciting tales of battle. Between them, he asked Ian about himself, even though the boy protested he had never done anything interesting, only lived in a little village and done his chores. But Gar pressed him for details anyway, and seemed fascinated by the homely accounts of Ian's boyhood friendships and conflicts, of his games and fights, of the holy day celebrations and the winters' tales against the darkness and the blizzards. Ian was reticent at first, but talked more and more easily as the sincerity of Gar's interest became apparent, until he was chattering away, warming to Gar's attention as a flower opens to the sun, until he found himself telling of his father's flogging and his own escape. Here Gar reined in the horses and dismounted to walk a while with his arm around the boy, saying little, but comforting him by his mere presence. When the tears had dried, Gar said gently, "What I can't understand is how you lasted through the first night, until I found you. Did you spend it all in the Stone Egg?"

"No, sir. I hid with the Little People."

"The Little People?" Gar looked up, startled. "Are they real, then?"

"Oh yes, sir!" Ian looked up at him, wondering

again how Gar could have lived all his life in this
land and not known so simple a thing. "They hid me
in their hall, but only for the one night—they feared
Lord Murthren's searchers would lead him to me,
and they would be discovered."

"So they fear the soldiers, eh?"

"Yes, sir."

"How is it I haven't seen them?"

Ian shrugged. "Because of that fear, sir. They hide
in their halls, and none see them unless the dwarves
themselves wish it."

"Well." Gar paced a moment in silence, then said,
"If you should chance to see them again, tell them I
said they have suceeded far better than they know."

Ian wondered at that, but knew better than to ask.
They mounted again, and rode on their way through
the night.

They came to Lord Aran's castle shortly after
dawn. The country was flat here, farmlands and
woodlots spreading out as far as the eye could see,
with no hill on which to build a castle—so Lord
Aran's stronghold sat in the middle of a cleared plain,
on an island in a small lake. The villages of his serfs
were scattered all about the shore, three or four of
them, and a score more out in the fields.

The castle itself was of granite, with four tall, bat-
tlemented towers around the squat central cylinder
of the keep, which rose high above the sixty-foot curtain wall. A long wooden causeway, built of timbers
a foot thick, stretched out to the castle, but stopped
twelve feet short of its gate, and the drawbridge that
made up the rest of its length was drawn up now.

There was another drawbridge at the shoreward end of the causeway; it too was drawn up.

Gar and Ian rode up to the shore opposite the drawbridge. Gar dismounted and said, "Out of the saddle, lad, and let your pony graze. We've a wait before us, till they open up for the day."

It was about half an hour before the castle's drawbridge came down with a clatter and a boom. Four soldiers rode out toward the shore. Their leader stiffened in his saddle as he saw Ian and Gar waiting on the shore. He waved to his companions, pointed ahead, and the four came onward at a trot.

"Into the saddle, lad." Gar swung aboard his tall roan. "They'll have a few words for us, you may be sure."

"Why?" Ian managed to mount his pony, still rather clumsy about it. "We've come to join them."

"They don't know that yet," Gar said, grinning. "For all they know, we could be spies disguised as soldiers, or renegade gentlemen fleeing from the law—or, for that matter, nothing but footsore, weary travellers who need a place to rest."

"Would travellers seeking rest come at daybreak?" Ian wondered.

"Probably not," Gar conceded, "so they'll think we're enemies, until we've proved otherwise. After all, who would ride by night, if he had nothing to fear?"

The drawbridge before them came down with a crash, and the guardsmen trotted across it. The one in the forefront leveled his pike and cried, "Friend or foe?"

"Friend," Gar replied. "I am Captain Gar Pike, a mercenary soldier, and this is Ian Tobinson, my apprentice. We seek employment with Lord Aran."

"Employment, eh? Looking for a job, is it? What worth to Lord Aran is a man who sells his sword?"

Gar's smile vanished. "You know our code—once we've accepted a man's coin, we are loyal till the battle is over."

"Aye," the lieutenant admitted, "but there are tales of blank-shield soldiers who have turned traitor for pay."

"And tales of other mercenaries, who rode them down and killed them for their treachery," Gar countered with a scowl. "Then too, I mind me an I have heard of no few serf-soldiers, and even gentlemen, who have done the same, though they fought for their own lord, and not for pay."

The lieutenant rested his hand on his sword and moved his horse closer. Gar touched his own sword. "It is not for you to judge my loyalty," he said softly, "nor to hire me or send me on my way. Your duty is only to bring me to your lord."

"Aye, and to clap you into irons if you are a traitor or a spy," the lieutenant snapped.

Gar slid his hand inside his doublet and brought out a roll of parchment. "Here is a testament from my last employer, Lord Gascoyne, attesting to my loyalty, and to my quality as a soldier. See there his seal!"

The lieutenant took the parchment, unrolled it, and looked at the drop of sealing wax with the imprint of Gascoyne's ring. He nodded reluctantly and handed it back. "Have you many such others?"

"Five," Gar answered, "and all of them speak of my virtue."

"Only five?" The lieutenant peered sharply at him. "You have not been a soldier long."

"I have not been a *free-lance* long," Gar corrected. "It is scarce a year since I left the private companies, where I gained my rank, and struck out on my own."

The lieutenant nodded slowly, frowning. "Blank-shield soldiers usually come in companies. There are few of you who ride alone."

Gar nodded, smiling. "Then you will understand why I have only five other testaments. From this, I gather that I must be the only blank-shield soldier who has come to Lord Aran's castle."

"And a fool you were to do it," the lieutenant blurted, then clamped his jaws shut, looking angry and downcast.

"True," Gar said, grimly nodding. "No mercenary soldier in his right mind would seek to join a side that has so small a chance of victory, and so great a chance of defeat."

"We will not be defeated!" the lieutenant cried. "We will defend my lord Aran to the death!"

"And so shall I," Gar said softly. "Lord Aran, alone of all the lords in this land, is as just and merciful as a lord should be."

The lieutenant frowned. "Strange words, from a man who fights only for money."

"Aye, and a strange lord's gentleman who is willing to die, to defend him! How many battles have you heard of, in which the *gentlemen* died?"

The lieutenant's mouth tightened. "Few."

Gar nodded. "The serfs die; occasionally a gentleman, by accident; and the lords, never, of course. Think you that I am so young that I do not know this rule?"

"Even as you say, Aran is a lord worth dying for," the lieutenant said, stone-faced. "But I was born and raised his man. You were not, and therefore must you be a fool."

"Indeed," Gar retorted, "for any *wise* gentleman would have ridden over this bridge, turned his coat, and sold his allegiance to one of the neighboring lords, so that he would be on the winning side when they come to fight Lord Aran."

The lieutenant's face darkened. "Do you say I am mad?"

"Mad as a hatter," Gar said cheerfully, "and so am I—and therefore have I come here to die with you."

The lieutenant's face lost some of its hardness, then grew somber. "It may be that we shall not die. It may be that Lord Aran shall prevail against those who seek to pull him down."

Gar sighed and shrugged. "It is possible," he agreed, "but scarcely likely."

"Aye," the lieutenant agreed. "It would take a miracle."

"Then it is for us to provide such a miracle." Gar grinned. "Come, Lieutenant. Take me to your lord."

The lieutenant stared, then finally smiled—but

Gar suddenly lifted his head, then turned to look off to the west. Ian looked too, but heard nothing.

Far away, a small dark line was crossing the horizon, reaching out toward the causeway.

"The serfs, with their wagons, livestock, and goods," Gar said softly. He turned back to the lieutenant. "I heard their carts creaking, far away. Will the battle be so soon as that?"

"So the reports do say." The lieutenant's face was set, grim. "The rival lords have assembled their armies. They may ride today; they may be at our gates at any time."

"It is well that I came when I did," Gar said.

The lieutenant turned his horse. "Follow," he said. "I will bring you to his lordship."

Gar turned to Ian. "You have heard of Lord Aran, lad. Would you like to meet him?"

Ian gulped and nodded.

The three serf soldiers turned their horses, encircling Ian and Gar from behind. The mercenary smiled and rode across the causeway toward the castle.

Ian followed.

As they rode down the long pier, Ian wrinkled his nose. The wood smelled abominably.

Gar saw his look and smiled. "It is pitch, lad. The boards are soaked with it. When the enemy comes, Lord Aran will burn this causeway."

Ian looked up at him, wide-eyed, then stared down at the blackened wood. His stomach twisted at the thought of the inferno to come—and twisted again as he realized what it meant: that anyone in the castle would be completely isolated from the shore. True, they might be safe in an impregnable fortress, able to thumb their noses at the world—but they might also be trapped.

They rode over the second drawbridge, under the huge iron spears of the portcullis, through a stone tunnel whose walls had arrow slits, and out into the bailey.

Ian looked around, amazed. He had never been inside a castle before, and could scarcely believe that so much land could be contained within a stone wall. It seemed far bigger than it had from the outside. But large as it was, there was a flurry of activity; soldiers were drilling in the center of the yard, gentlemen with swords were fencing with one another; servants hurried to and fro, marking out squares on the ground with powdered lime and bearing loads of straw to dump within those squares. Smoke streamed into the air from a low building against the western wall, and hammers rang within it—a smithy, Ian guessed, and the smith and his apprentices were making more weapons. A shiver ran down his back as he realized that he was going to be in the center of a battle—but if he wished to be a mercenary like Gar, he had better become accustomed to it.

Besides, he reflected, it was far better than staying on Lord Murthren's estates, and watching those he loved be scourged and beaten.

The thought brought memories of his father to mind; he shook them off and hurried after Gar.

They dismounted near the keep, and a hostler stepped forward to take their reins. Ian turned to follow the man, but the lieutenant called out, "Nay, lad!" and to Gar, "His lordship will wish to see the boy, too, if he is your apprentice."

Gar nodded to Ian, but the boy glanced at the horses, worried that he might not be doing his job.

"Don't worry, lad, I'll treat them well," the hostler said with a gap-toothed grin. "I'll leave the currying to you, though."

"Oh! Yes, sir! Thank you!"

But the man shook his head. "No 'sir,' lad—I'm but a serf, and you are a gentleman, or will be."

Ian swallowed hard, realizing that he had given himself away.

But the hostler hadn't noticed. "Go along with you, now," he said, and turned away, leading the horses. Ian turned to follow Gar and the lieutenant; he had to hurry, for they had gone ahead without him, assuming he would follow.

The lieutenant led them up a flight of stairs that curved against the side of the keep; another like it curved down from the landing before the great portal where two soldiers stood on watch. They struck their chests in salute as the lieutenant came up to them; he responded with a nod, and went in through the high, wide doorway.

They came into a large antechamber that seemed very dim after bright sunlight, but Ian could see benches around the walls, arms racked in brackets, and soldiers standing on guard at either side of an inner door, with a third by the stairway. He saluted as the lieutenant passed; the officer responded with a nod and led his guests up the narrow steps that curved to follow the wall of the keep. They passed two landings lighted by arrow-slits, then came into a wide hallway that ended in a large window filled with real glass. Sunlight streamed in, so Ian knew they must have gone a quarter of the way round the keep, and that the window would look out into the bailey, though from the side.

The lieutenant led them down the hall to a door guarded by two footmen. They struck their chests in salute; he responded with a nod. "Announce me to his lordship."

One of the guards went in and came back a few moments later. "His lordship will see you, Lieutenant."

They went in, and Ian stopped, staring at the white-haired, white-bearded man in a rich velvet robe who stood bending over a table, frowning down at its surface. A prickling passed over his head and down his back as he realized he was looking at Lord Aran himself, the man about whom stories were whispered between serfs indoors during the long winter evenings, stories that Ian had heard as long as he could remember, stories of mercy and justice and compassion—for serfs! For mere serfs, who were little better than most animals and worse than some, who had no right to expect such gentle treatment but received it anyway. No one knew why, but it was whispered that in his youth, Lord Aran had been in love with a beautiful serf who had died bearing him a child, and it was for her sake that he treated all his serfs as he had wished to treat her. Ian wondered if love could really make so huge a change in a man.

The old lord looked up. "Yes, and who is this, Lieutenant?"

"He is a free-lance, my lord—Captain Gar Pike and his apprentice Ian Tobinson, who wish to serve with you."

"Serve with me!" The old lord swung to Gar, frowning. "Die with me, you mean! Are you ready for that, gentleman?"

"If we must," Gar said, with a ghost of a smile. "But I would rather fight for you, my lord, and gain a victory."

"Victory!" The old lord slapped a hand on the table. "Come, look at this map and tell me the odds of victory!"

"I can tell you that from having ridden in, milord." But Gar came to the table and looked down at the chart. He pointed with a finger. "We halted awhile on this height, and I saw that it is a mile from your castle. Nothing but a cannon or an energy projector could reach you here."

The lord looked up sharply. "What know you of cannon and energy projectors?"

"I have fired cannon, and know them well. As to energy projectors, I know only what I have heard from officers who have survived them—or used them. They are said to throw lightning bolts for ten miles and more; cannon can hurl huge balls of lead at least as far."

"True, so far as it goes." The lord nodded. "And those weapons are, of course, the ones that I fear—those, and the flying boats that can hurl lightning at us from the skies."

"Flying boats?" Gar looked up, interested. "So the tales are true! But have you no concern about *floating* boats, milord?"

"Not greatly," Lord Aran said. "Even a catapult could sink one, and I have cannon of my own."

"Then what need to fear those of other lords?"

"Because cannon require gunpowder and leaden balls, young man, and projectors require energy. Those who besiege us may make as many of either as they wish, but we must make do with what we have within our walls."

Gar frowned down at the map. "How long will those endure?"

"Perhaps three months—perhaps less," the old lord said heavily.

Gar nodded. "Then we must break the siege at once, while we still have the ammunition to do it."

"And how shall you do that?" The old lord scowled.

"Why, by breaking their projectors and cannon." Gar grinned. "From what I have heard, they cannot make more."

The old lord just stared at him a moment, then slowly smiled. "Aye, they cannot. But how shall you break their pieces, young gentleman?"

"By very well-placed shots with cannon of your own, milord—or by small raiding parties who shall go by night with hammers and axes."

Lord Aran's smile stayed, even though he said, "It will take somewhat more than hammers and axes, Captain, and they who do the deed are like to die in the trying—but you give me hope. Yes, just the faintest glimmer—we may yet survive." He turned to the lieutenant. "Give him a coat of my cloth, my shilling for his pouch, and a troop of serfs to train." He turned back to Gar. "I know not what imp of perversity urges you to join with us, young gentleman, but I am glad of it."

Ian knew the name of that imp, though—Master Oswald.

They came back out into the courtyard, and Ian halted, amazed. The huge space seemed somehow dwarfed, for it was filled with a churning mob and a roaring of noise. Mothers called after their children, men yelled to one another, cattle bawled, sheep and goats bleated. Every serf on the estate must have been within those walls—or on his way; looking up, Ian saw that soldiers were hurrying new arrivals out of the way, so that more could stream in through the gatehouse tunnel.

"Lord Aran is serious," Gar said, gazing out over the mass of people. "The siege will begin soon."

"Not today," the lieutenant said grimly, "but the lords may well begin to move tomorrow. We must get this horde sorted out and bedded down before the enemy arrives at our walls." He called back through the doorway. "Corporal!"

A young man came out and saluted. "Sir!"

"This is Captain Pike," the officer said. "Conduct him and his apprentice to the barracks, then bring him to me; I'll be by the gate." He turned back to Gar. "Be as quick as you can; we will need your help in sorting out this mob."

"Why, then, I'll come now," Gar said, and turned to the corporal. "Show my apprentice where we'll be quartered, then take him to the stables. He'll take our saddlebags to the barracks, and he can show me there himself when the day's done." He turned back to Ian. "Curry the horse and pony first, lad, then stow the saddlebags. After that, go about where you may and make yourself useful. Good enough?"

"Aye, sir!" Ian said, though within, he trembled at the thought of being alone in the midst of such noise and such strangeness.

"Good lad. Enjoy the adventure." Gar grinned, clasped his shoulder, then turned to follow the lieutenant.

Ian swallowed heavily and turned to look up at the corporal. "Where are the barracks, sir?"

"Over there, against the south wall." The soldier pointed. "We'll follow the curve of the keep—that should get us out of the worst of the jostling. Come along, then." He strode off down the stair, and Ian hurried after him, his heart in his mouth.

CHAPTER
~10~

Gar had taught him how to use the curry comb, so Ian was able to see to both animals. He mucked out the horse's stall too, since no one had done so recently, then took the saddlebags back to the barracks.

He remembered the corporal's advice, though, so he stayed near the curtain wall, and did indeed move more quickly, even though the route was longer. When it joined the keep, he turned to follow that wall, so he passed by the stairs at the doorway again.

"Boy!"

Ian halted and looked around.

"Boy!" the voice called again, demanding. It was high-pitched and clear, an imperious treble. Looking up, Ian saw a girl about his own age leaning over the stone stair-rail. She wore rose-colored satin, and her skirts spread out in a prodigal display of cloth. "Come here, boy—I want you."

Ian swallowed and climbed the stairs toward her— she was clearly a gentleman's daughter, at least.

But as he came up to her, she smiled eagerly, and her voice dropped to a conspiratorial whisper. "Oh, good! I was hoping you would hear me!"

"Yes, miss—uh, ma'am . . . uh, 'selle . . . uh . . ."

She laughed, a clear cascade. "Oh, don't be so silly! Don't you know who I am?"

"No, miss . . . uh, ma'amselle . . ."

"Milady," she corrected, rather primly. "You must call me 'milady,' for I am Lord Aran's granddaughter, the Lady Heloise."

"Yes, milady," Ian said, relieved to know how to address her, and in a near-panic at the thought that he had made a mistake.

She saw his confusion and laughed again. "Oh, you must not worry so! I think it's all silliness anyway, these titles and bowing and all, especially since you're the first child I've seen in a year! You will play with me, won't you?"

Ian's heart sank; he had seen girls' games in his village, and didn't relish the thought of being a mock father to a doll. In a last, desperate attempt at salvation, he asked, "Wouldn't his lordship be angry?"

"Not at all, if I command you to do it." She glanced at the saddlebags. "But you're on an errand for your master, aren't you?"

"Yes, ma'am."

"Well, go do it, then come right back!" she said firmly. "And if anyone tries to stop you, tell them you're running an errand for the Lady Heloise!"

"Yes, milady! Surely, milady!" Ian bobbed his head and turned away in relief, but also in trepidation. There was hope, though—perhaps, before he came back, Heloise's mother would have found her and set her to her lessons or embroidery, or something.

He found out later that Lady Heloise didn't have a mother—the Lady Constantina had died not long after Heloise was born. She had died from nursing serfs—there had been an outbreak of disease, and she had caught it herself, on her errands of mercy. Heloise's father, Lord Aran's son, had died of a broken heart, some said—but others pointed out that he had devoted himself to the welfare of his people, working night and day to take care of the serfs in tribute to his wife's memory, and had died protecting them from robbers—though some said he had been hoping for death all along, not wanting to live without her.

All of that was in the future, though. For the present, Ian duly deposited the saddlebags beneath the bunk that would be Gar's, in the little private room at the end of the barracks, then dodged and twisted his way through the crowd (hoping it would take longer that way) and arrived back at the keep stairs, crestfallen to see the little figure in rose-colored satin still waiting for him.

Though, truth to tell, he could have been more crestfallen than he was. Heloise had long blonde hair, huge blue eyes, a button of a nose, and a wide, full-lipped smile. Ian couldn't help noticing the skip in his heartbeat, couldn't help thinking she was the most beautiful girl he had ever seen—but then, he reminded himself sternly, he had never seen a lady of his own age before.

"Come!" she demanded imperiously, and swept in through the keep door.

The conference of war was over; Lord Aran nodded at his captains and said, "To your places. They cannot be long now."

The officers bowed and turned to file out.

"Captain Pike," Lord Aran said, "remain a moment."

Magnus looked up, startled, then turned back to the white-haired nobleman, ignoring the jealous glances of the local captains. "Yes, my lord?"

Lord Aran glanced at the door, waited till it closed, then turned back to Magnus. "My granddaughter tells me that she commanded your apprentice to be her playfellow yesterday."

Magnus stood stock-still a moment, letting it register. Then he said, "Indeed, my lord!"

"Indeed," Aran confirmed. "I see the lad has not told you of this."

"No, my lord." Magnus could understand why.

"It will not, of course, interfere with his duties to you," Lord Aran said, "and I am glad to learn of it, for she has had few enough playmates in her life."

Magnus relaxed.

"Indeed, from her reports, he is a wondrously polite little fellow," the old lord said, "and quite attentive to her desires."

"I am glad to hear it," Magnus murmured.

Lord Aran nodded. "Still, I would wish that he were reminded not to forget his place."

Small chance of that, Magnus thought as he bowed his head in assent—but Lord Aran was thinking of Ian as a gentleman's son, not knowing that he was a serf, and overawed by nobility.

Lord Aran misinterpreted Magnus's expression. "No, no, do not misunderstand, he shows no sign of such impudence! But it would not hurt to remind him."

"I shall, my lord."

"It is well." Lord Aran relaxed. "Of course, with the battle come upon us, it does not grieve me to have a free-lance's apprentice near my daughter—she might give the slip to her bodyguards, but she would be apt to take him along."

Magnus smiled. "True, your lordship. I had not thought of that."

There was a commotion in the hall, and a sentry burst in. "My lord! They come!"

"To the battlements, at once!" Lord Aran strode out of the room. Magnus followed in his wake.

From the top of the keep, they could see the entire plain, with the ridge line to the southeast and the rocky outcrop to the north. Below them, the last few peasants were straggling across the drawbridge with their carts and livestock. Magnus knew they had been coming in all night, and that the causeway had been so jammed last evening that many of them had had to wait until it cleared. These were the last and most exhausted, and as they came, the draw-bridge rose behind them.

"Where?" Lord Aran demanded.

"Yonder, my lord!" The captain of the guard pointed. "From the southeast."

A file of men had begun moving down the slope.

Lord Aran nodded. "They will be here by sunset." He turned to his officers. "While we wait, drill your men. Warn them that there will likely be no work for them until the morrow—it would be a foolish enemy who would attack with tired troops."

The officers glanced at one another, then back at Lord Aran, waiting for the command that had not come.

"Be about it," Lord Aran said, with a slight smile.

"Yes, my lord!" The captains saluted and turned away.

But the enemy did not wait for the morrow—in the middle of the afternoon, a loud noise reached the sentries, and they sent for Lord Aran. Seconds later, a foot-thick ball of rock splashed into the lake not far from the drawbridge. A few minutes later, another explosion sounded, and hard on its heels, a ball crashed into the curtain wall. It bounced off with no damage they could see from the inside, but another followed it, and another.

Lord Aran came out into the battlements, saw a fourth ball hurtling through the air as the explosion echoed in the distance, and grunted. "Bombards," he said. "They are staying in period for the beginning, at least."

Puzzled frowns answered him, but Magnus knew what he meant. The enemy surely had modern big guns at their disposal, as well as energy projectors.

The ball cracked into the castle's granite and bounced into the lake.

"The wall will break if they keep that up long enough," Lord Aran said. He glared off toward the southeast. "Captain Pike, I hope you are as good as your word."

"Well, it may take me several shots, my lord." Magnus went over to one of the huge bombards that poked between crenels. "Load, men!"

A serf crew poured in gunpowder and heaved a ball into the cannon's mouth.

A distant boom sounded again.

Magnus looked up, gazing toward the southeast, then saw the speck of darkness appear against the sky. He gauged its trajectory and called, "Everyone down!"

"Clear the bailey!" a sentry bawled, and other voices took up the cry. Open space appeared in the center of the courtyard as if by magic, as serfs took cover against the walls—but in orderly fashion, with none in danger of being trampled.

Magnus was impressed. Lord Aran had good officers, who saw to it that there was good discipline.

The cannonball landed with a flat crack, burying itself in the turf of the parade ground.

Everyone was silent.

"How good of them to send us ammunition," Lord Aran rumbled.

A howl of laughter answered him, and the old lord smiled.

Grinning, Magnus turned back to his cannon, laying hold of the crank and raising the muzzle a touch, then cranking it around just a few minutes clockwise. It was all for effect, though—he had fired such antique bombards before, and knew they were scarcely precision instruments. He watched the horizon and saw a sudden puff of smoke. "Fire!"

A huge explosion rocked the battlements. The cannon slammed back against its chain, and smoke streamed out over the courtyard. Magnus waited for it to clear, gazing anxiously at the sky, trying to find his cannonball, hoping it hadn't gone astray.

There it was, diminishing even as he watched. He reached out to touch it with his mind, changing its trajectory just a little, feeling the pressure of wind against it, resisting. . . .

Another puff of smoke appeared on the horizon.

Magnus guided the ball straight toward the puff. It sank down right where the smoke had been. Whatever noise it made was too little to be heard from where they were, but Magnus felt the first stab of pain in the minds of the gunners before he managed to turn his attention away.

Lord Aran was staring after the ball. "I do believe you may have hit them."

"Or come close enough to scare them, at any rate," another captain said.

"I hit them," Magnus said, with grim certainty.

Another puff of smoke appeared—but quite some distance from the first.

A cheer went up from the battlements. "You hit them, you must have hit them!" The lieutenant slapped Magnus's shoulder, grinning. "Why else would a new gun answer us?"

The other was, indeed, silent.

The boom of the new gun sounded, and its ball splashed into the lake far from the castle.

"Loaded and ready, sir," the serf sergeant said.

Magnus nodded and cranked the gun around. "Fire!"

Another explosion rocked them, another cloud of smoke hid the climbing ball—but Magnus already had contact with it, was guiding its flight with telekinesis.

A puff of smoke appeared from the new gun, none from the old.

Magnus guided the ball right down on top of the smoke. At the last minute, he felt someone's relief that the ball would pass over the gun, and dropped it sharply. Again he felt a stab of pain and alarm, and closed off his mind.

"Again!" The lieutenant slapped his shoulder. "Two bombards out, with two shots! What a gunner you are!"

"Aye." Lord Aran fairly beamed at Magnus. "How do you manage such wonders, Captain Pike?"

"I learned calculus," Magnus explained—which was true, but really had very little to do with the issue.

The guns were silent for the rest of the day, and Magnus began to worry. What were they cooking up?

So he did a little mental eavesdropping—not unethical, since they were the enemy—and discovered that they were moving their energy projectors up. Yes, the projectors had greater range than the cannon—but they needed a clear line of sight, which the cannon did not, so they, too, had to be brought up to the ridge line. Magnus relaxed—he was fairly confident when it came to dealing with energy in any form.

The infantry pressed onward across the plain. Plumes of smoke began to appear, and the sentries reported it, grim-faced. The word spread to the peasants below, and women wailed and men cursed, for the smoke was that of their villages burning.

As dusk came, the army was only a mile away, and the plumes of smoke turned to the glow of flames. Lord Aran looked out across his ravaged estates and nodded grimly. "Fire the causeway."

Runners with torches sped out across the causeway to the bank, then came back, lighting the piles of tinder laid ready at the sides of the bridge. Flame-flowers blossomed behind them; then the pitch caught with a roar, and the landward drawbridge went up in a blaze. The flames raced toward the castle, a line of fire arrowing out toward the stronghold but stopping short where the drawbridge had been drawn up. Great clouds of greasy smoke filled the air, making the sentries cough and wheeze atop the battlements. Between fits, they stared, their isolation coming home to them at last—and serfs jammed the stairs, striving for a look, then passing word to their fellows below. " 'Tis a bridge of flames!" " 'Tis a curtain of fire!" " 'Tis as the Judgement Day itself!"

Then they fell silent, awed and shivering as they realized they were committed more fully than they had ever been.

Magnus knew that other lords might have left half their serfs or more to the mercy of the enemy—certainly the women, children, and old men, so that they would not be a drain on the castle's supplies—but Lord Aran cared for his people's welfare, and they cared for him in return.

"Let them make of that what they will, the nobles who beset our lord!" one captain said stoutly.

"What do they think, I wonder?" a lieutenant answered.

But Magnus knew. The lords had been sure Aran would burn his bridges, and the gentlemen had suspected it—but the serfs in the ranks were awed and fearful at the sight, so reminiscent of the Hell of which their preachers had told them.

Then lightning struck, horizontal lightning, stabbing out across the plain to score the curtain wall with a huge thunder-crack, echoing for seconds, away to the ridge line.

Women screamed, serfs howled, all dove for cover. " 'Tis the anger of God!"

"Or the spite of the lords!" Magnus bellowed in answer, ducking down behind a wall. "Only of the noblemen who would bring down our Lord Aran for his charity!"

He knew he had at least thirty seconds, probably a few minutes—the energy projectors might be antiques, were certainly anything but state-of-the-art; their capacitors would need time to recharge—that is, if there were only one, yet; it would be quite like these spiteful aristocrats to start hurling lightning bolts the second they could, rather than waiting till all their forces were in place. Peering over the wall, he probed with his mind toward the ridge, listening for the gunners' thoughts.

There! The officer in charge of the energy projector, thinking about his task, preening himself on having hit the castle wall with his first shot. But he was thinking about his other artillery pieces, too. Sure enough, there was only the one gun in place, though there were seven more coming.

Seven! Magnus could see he was going to have a busy night. He probed the projector to see if it was constructed as he had thought. But he found no capacitor; this projector wasn't working on electricity! There was a battery, true, but it only fed current to the coils that lined the barrel, to direct the beam— and at the base of that tube was the open mouth of a plasma bottle, a set of extremely powerful magnetic fields that held in a plasma of ionized hydrogen and heated it to the point of fusion! The idiots had brought an H-bomb to discipline their renegade member; they had brought a sun to earth! Plasma cannon were for space heaters, not for surface warfare!

One way or another, he had to disable that monster. He followed the circuits, found and traced the huge cable that led to the power source—a fission reactor, heavily shielded. The idiots! If that shielding cracked, they could die of radiation poisoning.

No. Serfs would die, gentlemen would die—but lords wouldn't go anywhere near that thing.

Grimly, Magnus speeded up molecules inside a current-bearing wire. They grew hotter and hotter, melting insulation, flowing, touching the ground wire . . .

He felt the shock, both from the electrical explosion he had triggered and from the minds of the men near it. There was a raw, mental scream of pain—one serf had been burned—but the gentleman was only surprised at the short circuit, then suddenly afraid of what would happen when the lord found out. He began to snap out quick orders to disconnect the cable and begin repairs.

Magnus relaxed; they weren't exactly long on skilled labor, these people. It would be an hour or more before that gun could work again—and it wouldn't last that long. He rose from his crouch and nodded to his gun crew. "Ready?"

"Loaded and waiting, sir." But the serfs stayed down below the wall, staring at him with huge, frightened eyes.

"Good." Magnus turned cranks, shifting the gun's aim slightly, then stopped back and nodded to the lieutenant. "Fire."

The man jumped up, touched his match to the hole, and dropped back down below a crenel as the gun blasted. Magnus stayed on his feet, knowing he had nothing to fear, narrowing his eyes as he watched the ball arc away toward the ridge, adjusting its flight, guiding it with faint nudges. . . .

There was a flare of light on the horizon, and men-

tal shrieks of alarm and fright, then a black anger
from the gunnery officer—and relief; he wouldn't
have to try to explain that short circuit, after all.

Magnus smiled, finding satisfaction in the irony of
an antique bombard taking out a high-technology
energy projector.

"What . . . what was that flare, Captain?" the lieutenant asked.

"You know full well, Lieutenant," Magnus answered with asperity. "It was the energy projector
being crushed." He turned to the Officer of the Watch.
"We won't have to worry about that gun again—but
they'll bring in others. It's going to be a long night."

"Not if you can shoot that well with all the others,
Captain," the man said with a grin.

"Only when I've light—it will be much more difficult at night."

The officer's smile vanished. "So, of course, they
will wait till night to give us any more bolts."

"Quite likely," Magnus agreed, "so I'm going to
the barracks to catch some sleep, while I can—it's
going to be a long watch from dusk till dawn. Wake
me if there's any sign of trouble, will you?"

"Oh, you may be sure of that!"

"Thank you." Magnus smiled and turned away.

Serf eyes tracked him as he came down the stairs—
then, all about him, the simple folk began to relax,
and turned to salvaging what they could of their
tents and lean-tos. Women lighted their fires and
went back to preparing the evening meal. Magnus
looked about him as he walked to the barracks,
amazed at the resiliency of these people, who so

quickly began to re-establish some semblance of normality. Of course, they were descended through generations of folk who had done the same down through the centuries, through wars and natural disasters; they had learned to take advantage of the peaceful moment, when it came. For folk still had to eat, and still needed shelter and warmth, and took as much of it as they could when they could, for who knew when it would come again?

In the dark of the night, lightning bolts stabbed all at once and from every direction—north, south, east, west, points in between, and two from straight overhead.

"Down!" Magnus shouted, taking cover behind the curtain wall, but his yell was drowned by the thunder of the energy projectors, then by the chorus of screams as peasant tents and lean-tos blazed. The smell of burning flesh rose in the air, smoke boiled forth, and the lightnings stabbed again with the thunder about them. By their light, Magnus saw boats shooting out from the shore, crammed with quaking serf soldiers whose sergeants drove them with whips while officers stood behind with muskets, ready to kill any sergeant who hesitated.

Then he had to duck down again—and this time, he sought with his mind. Moral qualms had drowned in screaming, and the time for deftness and delicacy was past. He probed into the engine of the flier overhead and wrenched. Above him, he heard an explosion; then a meteor plunged toward the lake, spitting fire. He let it go, searched, found the other, and gave it the same treatment. As soon as he heard the explosion, his mind was out and questing toward the horizon, orienting on the mind of a gunner, then sliding into the machine he tended, altering the angle of a coil so that the magnetic bottle inside tilted, its mouth swerving against the side of the breech, instead of being open to the muzzle. . . .

A miniature sun rose on the ridge line, and the gunners' thoughts ceased. Then a huge explosion echoed about them all, and Magnus's mind was out and searching for the next gun. Once again a bottle tilted, plasma fused into helium, and a new sun lit the night.

CHAPTER
~11~

Men ran to and fro across the battlements, but Magnus ignored them, searching for the next projector and the next. He was sure the courtyard was filled with screaming, but he couldn't hear it through the thunder that filled the night around him. Gun after gun exploded, the echoes of one blast only slightly beginning to diminish before the next crashed out, and the night was bright with hellfire and slashed with shadow.

Then the last energy projector was gone, but the blazing light still lit the night, from glowing mushroom clouds that merged above. The thunder rumbled away and died, and finally Magnus could hear the screaming—but also the shouting and cursing from the lake, as terrified sergeants drove their crews onward toward the castle. Magnus knew that a huge trough now ringed the plain, and hoped the idiot lords had had sense enough to use clean fusion cannon. He hoped some of them had been near enough to be caught in the fireballs.

"What has happened! What have they done!" It was Lord Aran, disheveled and in deshabille, obviously having yanked on whatever clothes had come to hand. He came striding out onto the ramparts, calling for information.

Magnus ran up to him. "They surrounded us with energy projectors, my lord, including two fliers overhead, and all blasted at us at the same moment."

"We must shoot back! To the cannon!"

"We have, my lord," Magnus said, lying only a little, "and their guns are silenced—but their soldiers come."

"To the guns again! Sink their boats!"

"They are too close, my lord, and too many!" Magnus shouted to be heard over the din. "See!"

He pointed at the lake. The old lord looked, and the blood drained from his face. He saw his castle encircled by boats, three concentric rings of them, the nearest only a hundred yards away—and huge gaping breaches in his wall. His face calmed with the resignation of the doomed, and he laid his hand on his sword. "Then we must fight till we die."

"No, my lord!" Magnus shouted. "We must flee! They will not harm your serfs or gentlemen, for they've done nothing wrong—only obeyed their lord, as they must. But you they will execute. Away! It is far more important to your people, to all the people of this benighted world, that you live, so they may know there is still a champion of their rights somewhere!"

"Rights?" Lord Aran turned to stare at him. "What word is that?"

"It means charity for serfs! Protection from wanton cruelty! The chance to become happy! It means life! So long as you live, so does that dream! My lord, come away!"

"But . . . how?" Lord Aran looked about him, a lion at bay, for the first time uncertain.

"Never mind how!" Magnus swung hard. His fist cracked into the lord's jaw, and the old man folded.

Magnus dropped down and caught him over his shoulder. Grabbing hand and foot in a fireman's carry, he hurried down the stairs and through the nightmare.

"Grandfather!"

Magnus heard it with his mind, not his ears—they were too filled with the roaring of the flames and the screaming of the serfs. He looked back and up, and saw the small white gauzy form at the door to the keep. Beside her, there was a fainter glow—a boy's face. "Ian!" he called, knowing his voice would not reach and projecting it mind to mind. "Bring the Lady Heloise! Follow!" For of course, he could not leave the heir—the other lords would need to wipe out Aran's heresy, root and branch.

The blur that was Ian's face jerked as though it had ben slapped; then the girl was stumbling toward the steps as though someone were pulling her, and the boy's face floated before her as he struggled to follow.

Magnus turned away, thanking his stars for the one that had led him to Ian, and wormed and jostled his way through the throng toward the postern gate.

None sought to block his way; there was too much confusion. No one could take the time to see who he carried.

Then, suddenly, a tatterdemalion figure rose up in his path. "Gar! Stop!"

Magnus jarred to a halt, staring in disbelief at the motley tunic with the patchwork robe. "Siflot! What the hell are *you* doing here!"

"Message from Allouene!" the juggler yelled. "She says to get out fast! And whatever you do, don't try to save Lord Aran! He has to be a martyr!"

Magnus just stared at him, appalled. Then he called, "Siflot! Can you honestly believe that this fine old man *deserves* to die?"

The vagabond stared back at him—until his gaze faltered. "I cannot."

"Then stand aside! Or help me—but get out of my way!" Magnus bulled his way through, and somehow, Siflot wasn't there anymore. But the postern gate opened just before Magnus reached it, and Siflot was in the boat to catch the unconscious lord as Magnus lowered him in, then gone again as Magnus stepped down—but Ian shouted behind him, and Lady Heloise squealed, "Who did that?"

Turning, Magnus saw them in the boat and grinned. "Did what, chil . . . milady?"

"Dropped me into the boat!"

"Oh, that." Magnus turned to cast off the ropes. "Your guardian angel, milady."

"My angel?" She looked around, wide-eyed. "Where is she?"

"Well, perhaps not an angel," Magnus allowed as

he took up the oars, "but surely your guardian. If you ever meet a patchwork man who plays the flute and trips over his own feet while he juggles, trust him with your life."

Lady Heloise glanced about. "I see no such man here."

Magnus looked up, startled, but sure enough, there was no sign of Siflot. Another boat was moving away from the postern's water stairs, though, and Magnus realized his friend was taking out water-accident insurance. "No, but he'll be there when you need him," he cried. "Down, now, children! Our enemies must not see you!"

He ducked down himself, and stayed that way, ostensibly rowing by feel, actually moving the boat by telekinesis and probing the night with telepathy. It seemed to take a century, but he wound them unseen through the cordon, then out across the dark lake, shushing the children periodically in a lightless, interminable journey. Halfway through it, there was stirring and clunking in the boat, and Lord Aran's voice said thickly, "What . . . where . . .?"

"Grandfather!" Lady Heloise cried, but Magnus called out in a whisper, "Quietly, milady, quietly! My lord, be silent, I beg of you! We are on the lake, in the midst of your enemies!"

Aran was silent a moment. Then, "My serfs," he groaned.

"They are as well as they would be if we had died for them, my lord," Magnus pointed out. "In any case, we can do no more for them—save to keep their hopes alive, by keeping you alive! Softly, now, I beg!"

Then the old lord was quiet, but Magnus was sure he was awake—with an aching head and jaw. Magnus hoped the old man could overlook the blow of mercy.

Finally, the bottom of the boat ploughed into mud with a sucking noise, and the bow thudded against a bank. Magnus rolled out, stepped down through two feet of water into muck that swallowed his foot— and ankle, and calf, but not fast enough to keep him from throwing his upper body onto the bank. He clawed at grass, pulled his foot free, and rolled onto the turf with a gasp of relief. Then he reached out for the gunwale, but it wasn't there. "Ian!" he cried in desperation. "Take my hand!" He groped blindly in the dark—but a small hand caught his, and pulled with amazing strength for its size. "Here, Master Gar! What shall I do?"

"Why, just as you *are* doing," Magnus assured him. "Keep pulling, lad—there! I've caught the gunwale!" He turned about, holding the boat with both hands against the bank. "Out, now, but help the lady first!"

Heloise stepped out onto the bank, steadying herself on Ian's shoulder. Then the boy climbed out and turned back to hold out his hand. "My lord?"

"Thank you, boy." Aran steadied himself with Ian's hand as he climbed out. "Strong as a serf, you are! Your mother should be proud!" He turned toward Magnus. "All right, mercenary—you have saved me, whether I would or no. But I am grateful, for I would not leave my granddaughter alone in this world. Now where shall we go?"

"To shelter, my lord." Magnus climbed to his feet and looked down at Lord Aran. "There we shall rest, and consider what we may do. Ian!"

"Yes, sir!"

"We're going to try to travel by night, boy, and there's an outside chance that we might become separated. If we do, stay with the Lady Heloise at all costs! Do you understand? Guard her at whatever price you must—from this time until we reach safety, your life is hers. If we're attacked, your first task is to get her to safety; your second task is to fight any who attack her. Is that clear?"

"Yes, sir." Ian's eyes were huge in the night. "I shall guard her with my head."

"Good." Magnus nodded, satisfied with both meanings of the phrase. He clapped Ian on the shoulder. "Stout fellow! For now, follow." He turned away, offering the old lord his arm.

Privately, he wondered where Siflot was. He couldn't really ask the vagabond to actively help Lord Aran escape, since that was flatly against Alloucne's orders, and would jeopardize Siflot's whole career. But he was grateful to his friend, already.

They moved out across the plain; campfire coals glowed sullenly ahead. They had a camp to traverse. As silently as possible, Magnus threaded his way between tents, hoping against hope that all of the soldiers were in the boats.

They weren't.

A trooper rose up in front of them, staring, amazed. He was just beginning to open his mouth in alarm when Magnus's hand closed around his throat. His fist slammed into the man's jaw, and the soldier's eyes rolled up as he dropped.

But another soldier saw and howled, "Enemy! Captain of the Guard! They're upon us!"

Magnus leaped to the side and felled the man with a chop—but an avalanche of bodies hit, and bore him to the ground, kicking and punching. He surged back up, throwing men off him like a bear rising from its winter's sleep, and saw Lord Aran fencing with expert skill against two young officers. Magnus slammed heads, kicked bellies, and troopers fell around him. A club swung at his sinuses, but he leaned aside. It exploded like fire against his ribs, but he held his breath as he caught it and yanked; its owner stumbled after it, and Magnus felled him with a chop. A sword stabbed toward him, but he knocked it aside with the club.

Then the second wave hit.

It hit, but it fell back remarkably quickly. Magnus chopped and punched, rolling with the blows and striking back—and suddenly, he was standing, his head swimming, chest heaving, looking about at a score of fallen men . . .

And a tattered jester with a quarterstaff in his hands.

Magnus grinned and stepped forward to clap his friend on his shoulder. "Prince of jesters! You stood by me after all!"

"You and the lord," Siflot returned, grinning. "Your cause is just, for the lord is, too."

"Is just?" Magnus smiled, amused. "But your carecr, Siflot! If you help me keep him alive, Oswald will have your hide!"

"No, he won't," the jester said, with remarkable assurance, "though I don't doubt he'll try. The career can go hang, Gar—I never wanted it."

"Then what did you want with SCENT?"

"Why, to help people who needed it most." Siflot turned to Lord Aran with a bow. "And at the moment, Your Lordship, that is yourself."

"I thank you, Fool," Lord Aran panted. Then suddenly, his eyes went wide, and he looked about him in a panic. "My grandaughter! The Lady Heloise! Where is she?"

Magnus looked about too, suddenly realizing that the old lord had an Achilles' heel.

"I saw two small things go flitting away over the plain as I came to join you," Siflot said, "though truth to tell, the lady did not seem to be all that willing."

Lord Aran sagged with relief. "Yes, Captain Pike— you did bid the boy take her to safety." He looked up, still alarmed. "But how shall we find them now?"

"He will find us as easily as we him," Magnus answered. "She could have no better guide when it comes to running and hiding. Still . . ." He turned to Siflot with a surge of relief; he had found one solution to two problems—how to find the children, and how to keep Siflot from active involvement in his own crime. "Siflot, would you go search out the nooks and crannies, and bring them back to us?"

"Why, I will try," Siflot said slowly, "but even if I find them, they may not come to me."

Magnus remembered something that he had said half seriously, and grinned. "I told them that if they found a ragtag jester who played the flute and tripped over his own feet while he juggled, they were to trust him with their lives."

Siflot answered his grin. "Why, I think I can do all that, though perhaps not at once. May you fare well, my lord! We shall meet you anon!" He started away, then swung around on one foot and turned back. "Where are you bound, by the way?"

Magnus glanced at Lord Aran, and the answer sprang full-blown into his head. "Castlerock, Siflot! The island in the inland sea, where all the serfs have fled!" He turned back to Lord Aran. "You will be safer there, my lord, than any place else in this world! Will you go?"

"Aye, willingly," the old lord said slowly. "The escaped serfs might welcome me, might they not? Now that I, too, am a fugitive."

"They might," Magnus agreed. "Then, ho! Off to Castlerock!"

He turned away, and Lord Aran gasped beside him. "The jester—where did he go?"

"Oh, Siflot?" Magnus shrugged. "It doesn't matter. He'll find your granddaughter, my lord, and my apprentice—and they couldn't be in safer hands. He will assure the Lady Heloise that her grandfather is well, and will meet her at Castlerock. You would not want him to tell an untruth, would you?"

"No, surely not," said Lord Aran, with the ghost of a smile. "I suppose that, after all, I shall have to live, shan't I? To Castlerock!"

But they underestimated their enemies. Perhaps
Magnus should not have stolen the two horses—or
perhaps the soldiers they had vanquished gave the
alarm when they came to. At any rate, Magnus and
Lord Aran had only an hour's grace before the sounds
of dogs echoed in the distance, and a new moon
glided across the heavens, coming from the camp.

"A flier with a searchlight!" Magnus cried, glancing over his shoulder. "Ride, my lord! We're nearly to
the trees!" And he slapped the rump of Lord Aran's
horse.

"What good will the forest do?" Lord Aran called
over the pounding of hooves. "The hounds will still
follow our scent!"

"Perhaps, but their flier won't do them much
good. Quickly, my lord! At least give them a race!"

Then the trees were closing about them, and Magnus reined in. "Dismount, my lord!" He swung
down off his horse.

"Why?" Lord Aran dismounted even as he asked.
"What good will it do? Will we not still need the
horses?"

"No, my lord, for they can't go any faster than we,
in underbrush—and if we use the forest trails, they'll
find us in an instant!" He turned his horse about,
shouted and spanked it, and the horse broke out of
the forest with a startled whinny. Lord Aran imitated
him, and the two horses together fled out over the
plain.

The flier veered to follow them.

"That will not buy us much time," Lord Aran said,

but he was turning his back on the plain even as he said it.

"True," Magnus agreed. "They'll catch up to the beasts in a few minutes, and see the saddles are empty. Then they'll start combing the wood for us—but in that few minutes, we can become very thoroughly lost."

"I am already," Lord Aran grunted. "Have you any idea where you're going?"

"Toward the center of the wood, my lord. The thicker the trees, the better our chances. Have you ever hunted the fox?"

"Why of course!" Lord Aran looked up, startled. "Many, many times!"

"Then think like a fox, my lord, for you are in his place right now, with the hounds baying after you, leading the lords on their horses. Where would a fox hide?"

"In a dozen places, but ever on the move." Lord Aran grunted. "I take your meaning, Captain—and you may take the lead."

They plowed on through the night, breathing in hoarse gasps, thorns and briars tearing their clothing. After half an hour's movement, they began to hear the hounds again; ten minutes more, and the baying was closer.

"Into the stream!" Magnus jumped into the water. "Break our scent-trail!"

The old lord jumped in after him—and stumbled and fell. Magnus was by his side in an instant, hauling him back to his feet—but the old lord still sagged. Magnus hauled an arm about his neck, pushed a shoulder under Aran's, and half-dragged him along the stream bed, looking frantically for a hiding place. Aran was spent, and Magnus, to tell the truth, wasn't feeling terribly energetic himself.

The hounds' voices became louder, closer, then suddenly broke into a quandary of baying. Magnus knew they had found the end of the trail, and that their masters would realize the fugitive lord had fled into the stream. They would be fanning out to either side, searching both upstream and downstream. . . .

He began to hear voices calling, excited, hoarse. The excitement of the hunt was catching up even the serfs who had revered Lord Aran from the tales of his kindness and justice. Where, where could they hide?

A huge branch overhung the river. Magnus was tempted, and would have tried it if he'd been alone, but he knew he couldn't haul the old lord up there. He kept wading, his legs growing more and more weary, and voices began to echo from the other bank of the stream, coming closer. They would be on him in a minute! Good or bad, they must find a hiding place, now!

"Go to . . . ground," the old lord wheezed.

Magnus nodded; like a fox, they had to hide, and soon. "I'm looking for . . . a bolt-hole . . . my lord." For the first time, he began to think seriously of calling for his spaceship, and to hell with what it did to the mission by letting the lords know that someone else who knew about modern technology was active on the planet.

Then, suddenly, the trees on the left bank fell

away into a small meadow. Magnus looked up in a panic—the first forester who came into that clearing would see them! He definitely had to call for Herkimer, *now*. . . .

Then he saw the ovoid shape in the middle of the meadow.

A stone egg! He remembered the one Ian had come out of, remembered what Allouene had told him about the Safety Bases. He waded out of the river, hauling Lord Aran. "We have found it, my lord!"

The old man looked up, blinking. "What . . . ?"

"A Safety Base!" Magnus knelt slowly, lowering Lord Aran with him.

"But how . . . why . . . ?" Panic tinged the old lord's voice. Could it be, Magnus wondered, that he didn't know about these stations?

He remembered what Ian had told him of his fall into the egg, and pressed along the edge, trying to find the hidden hatch.

"We are lost," Lord Aran moaned, and slumped against the side of the rock. Then his moan turned into a cry of alarm as the surface gave way beneath him, and he fell into the hole.

Magnus leaped in after him, not giving the hatch time to close. Maybe it was keyed only for people of the right genetic makeup, maybe Lord Aran had just been lucky—but Magnus wasn't questioning good fortune.

The hatch closed above him, lights sprang to life, and Magnus, in a panic, called out, "No beacon! We need only rest, not rescue! Don't send for help!"

"As you wish, sir," a cultured voice replied. "Welcome to Safety Base 07734. What services will you require?"

"Only rest, food, and drink!" Magnus panted. "Thank you, Safety Base."

"We exist to serve," the computer's voice answered, then was silent.

Lord Aran looked about him, wide-eyed. "A Safety Base! Praise heaven!"

Then he collapsed into unconsciousness. Magnus was very glad—he was quite willing to wait, before Lord Aran started thinking of the inconvenient questions. He stooped to catch the old nobleman in a fireman's carry again, bore him down the spiral stairs to the nearest couch, then pulled off his boots, stripped off his wet clothes, wrapped him in a blanket, and propped his head on a pillow. That done, he straightened up with a sigh of relief, gazed a moment at his charge, then began to strip his own clothes off as he went into the bedroom, and just managed to aim himself toward a bed before fatigue took him and he fell.

Magnus awoke, bleary-eyed and aching. Looked around him and saw carpet, plasticrete walls, and viewscreens; he felt the smoothness of synthetics beneath his cheek—then suddenly remembered that he was on a medieval planet. Alarm sent him bolt-upright—had they been captured, or . . . ?

Then he remembered the end of the chase, the stone egg, the Safety Base, and went limp with relief. He hauled himself to his feet, stepped out of the bedroom, and saw the old lord still asleep on the couch.

Magnus nodded and went softly past him, knelt to pick up his clothes, and found them almost dry. How long had he slept?

He carried the clothes into the plush parlor and pulled on doublet and hose. Then he went up the winding stairs, stepped over to the control console, and asked, "How much time has elapsed since our entrance?"

"Ten hours, sir," the dulcet tones answered him.

Ten hours! Magnus wondered what Siflot and the children had been doing in that time. Were they still free? "You did not activate the beacon."

"No, sir. You had commanded otherwise."

Well, that was a mercy. "News scan, please. Have there been any broadcasts?"

"A constant exchange of information, sir. Lord Aran's castle has fallen, his estates and serfs are being divided up between his neighbors, and the search for him continues."

"To no avail?"

"No, sir. His trail ended not far from this station."

Magnus stiffened. "Where are they searching now?"

"In a spiral, sir, its center the point at which the trail ceased. The spiral has expanded to a diameter of five miles."

That was quick progress; they couldn't have been searching too thoroughly. Still, it gave Magnus a pang of anxiety for Siflot and the two children, if they had come as far as the forest. "Have they discovered any fugitives?"

"No, sir."

That was a relief, but it wasn't conclusive—if they'd caught the vagabond and the children, they might or might not have reported in by radio. On the other hand, who would think anything of a vagabond with two peasant children? Surely Siflot would think to disguise Heloise. Magnus relaxed, enough to realize how hungry he was. "Menu, please. Breakfast."

"Yes, sir. Our resources are limited; we can only provide steak and eggs, ham and eggs, several cereals, and rolls."

"Steak and eggs, please. And coffee." Magnus had learned to drink that beverage on Maxima, though he still wasn't certain he was happy about it.

A chime sounded below him. Going back down the stairs, he saw a steaming platter of eggs and brown meat on a small table, flanked by silverware. He crossed to it in two strides and sat down in one movement. The aroma was heavenly. He picked up a fork and started work.

Twenty minutes later, he decided it was time for a reconnaissance. With a sigh, he went up the stairs, pulled on his boots—and winced; they were still damp—then asked softly, so as not to wake Lord Aran, "Are there any enemies in the vicinity?"

"Define 'enemies.' "

Magnus bit his tongue; he didn't doubt that the computer knew what the word meant. It just wanted to know which side was which. Under the circumstances, since the lords were always the home team, he decided to drop the issue. "Are there any other human beings nearby?"

"Yes, sir. There is a woman twenty meters from this station."

Magnus froze. A woman? Who . . . ?

Somehow, he thought he knew.

Magnus stepped out of the hatch; it remained slightly ajar behind him, as he had told it to—not that he really thought he would need a quick escape route, but he was growing very cautious. He stepped forward, hands on hips, feet wide apart, and looked about him, upward, breathing deeply of the fragrances of the forest, like a man enjoying a beautiful morning—and it wasn't terribly hard to pretend just that, though it was mid-afternoon.

She stepped forward from a screen of brush, lissome and lithe, as beautiful in a medieval gown and bodice as she had been in tights and jacket. But her face wasn't anywhere nearly as attractive when it was set in such stony anger.

Magnus glanced her way, then bowed his head gravely. "Good afternoon, Lieutenant."

"Don't give me 'good afternoon,' recruit!" Allouene advanced on him, eyes blazing. "Do you realize just what a churned-up mess you've made of things?"

"Not really," Magnus answered, slowly and deliberately. "The castle fell, as you intended it to."

"Yes, but we had to get an agent in to suggest strategy, after you shot out those first three cannon! You *know* you weren't supposed to use modern sighting equipment!"

Magnus just stared. "*You* told the lords to surround the castle with energy projectors and fire all at once?"

"Not me—Oswald," she said impatiently. "And he had the devil of a time getting into the camp and dreaming up a pretext to mention the notion, I can tell you!"

"So SCENT is responsible for the deaths of all those serfs."

Allouene shrugged impatiently. "It would have happened eventually anyway—and as soon as we saw you were bound and determined not to let events take their course, we had to stop you, fast! How the hell did you blow up all those energy projectors, anyway?"

"A man who tries to use nuclear power as a weapon is a fool," Magnus said evenly. "So you couldn't take the chance that Aran might have been able to hold out."

"He couldn't possibly have lasted! It was just a matter of time before the other lords would squash him! The most he could hope for was martyrdom, so his example might inspire other men!"

"Or scare them off," Magnus said evenly. "Besides, there was his granddaughter. Would you have left her an orphan? Or were you planning on her being martyred, too?"

"Don't get smart with me, recruit! No matter how much you think of yourself, you're just a bare beginner! You can't possibly know anything about social change, beyond what I've taught you!"

"Don't be so sure of that," Magnus retorted, "but

true or not, I still know something of loyalty, and morality."

"The ends justify the means, Gar! You know that!"

"The ends do *not* always justify the means," he contradicted. "You must have a sense of proportion, a sense of balance."

"It's doctrine!"

"Doctrine by its nature is fallible. When it becomes inflexible, it opens itself to mistakes. You can't live your life by principles alone; you have to have compassion, too. If you don't, the best principles in the world can be corrupted into inhumanity. It's people who matter, not causes."

"If you honestly believe that, you can go someplace else to try to put it into practice!" Allouene snapped. "This is our planet, and we'll push it toward democracy as we see fit! And so will you! You took an oath, and you're under military discipline!"

"The oath I took was for the good of the people of the planets that SCENT would work on," Magnus said evenly, "and the miliitary can only apply discipline through a court-martial."

"We'll convene one."

"You'll have to start without me, then."

Allouene reddened, about to make another retort, but caught herself at the last instant. She took a deep breath, and forced a smile. "Look, Gar. The situation isn't totally fouled up yet. We can still salvage something. Leave the old lord to his own devices. His peers will catch him and try him, and he'll still be a martyr. Not as effective as dying in battle, but still good enough."

"And the child Heloise will still be alone in the world. And I will be have lost my honor, and have to live with the knowledge that I abandoned a man to whom I had sworn loyalty. No."

"Loyalty! Honor! You talk like somebody out of the Middle Ages!" Allouene snapped. "What have you done, gone native?"

"Let us say that I can understand the frame of reference," Magnus said, poker-faced.

"Then remember this—you swore loyalty to us first!" Allouene blazed. "You have no *right* to louse up our plans this way!"

"And you have no right to interfere with these people and their society. If you're going to do it at all, you should do it ethically."

"There are no ethics when it comes to trying to change a society!"

"There are," Magnus said. "You might start with trying to shorten the sufferings of the oppressed."

"We can't free them right away without starting a civil war! Even if they won and the lords were muzzled, the gentlemen and serfs don't know enough to establish a viable democracy! They don't even have the concept of human *rights* yet! Anything they build will fall apart! You'll have anarchy! Warlords fighting it out! *Everybody* will suffer!"

"But you can save the ones who are in the worst trouble in the meantime," Magnus retorted. "I won't try to upset your plans, Lieutenant Allouene—but I won't abandon this old lord, either."

"You already *have* upset our plans. And how do you think you can save that old lord, anyway?"

"I'll find a way," Magnus answered.

Allouene suddenly calmed, watching him narrow-eyed. "No, you won't—you already have, haven't you? You're too sure of yourself for anything else. You think you've figured out a way to save him! How?"

Magnus stood silent.

"Castlerock!" Allouene erupted. "You're planning to take him to Castlerock!"

"An interesting idea," Magnus replied.

"You fool, don't you know you'll never make it? It's seventy miles to that inland sea! With a hundred lords and all their dogs and all their men in between!"

"There will be long odds, no matter what I do," Magnus returned.

But the implications were just hitting Allouene. Her eyes widened in horror. "Damn! Castlerock, with all its escaped serfs, hit with a folk-hero like Lord Aran? You really do want to start that civil war, don't you?"

"Revolution," Magnus corrected, "and I don't think it will start for several generations yet."

"Castlerock can't hold out for several years, let alone several generations! The lords will concentrate all their firepower on it! They can't let it stand, especially not with Lord Aran there! The serfs will *have* to fight!"

"You could persuade the lords to ignore them," Magnus said softly.

"Ignore them? Can you ignore a live hand grenade under your dinner table? They can't allow it! *We* can't allow it!" Then Allouene caught her breath, realizing what she had said.

So did Magnus. "Try to stop me," he said.

Allouene's eyes narrowed. "We will."

CHAPTER
~12~

They tried. Oh, nothing overt—they couldn't let their intervention be obvious, after all—but Oswald had recruited dozens of locals as his agents before Allouene and her team ever arrived, and had several in the lords' camp; he saw to it that word of the fugitives' whereabouts leaked to the noblemen.

Magnus, however, made sure he and Lord Aran weren't there.

Oh, there were times when he couldn't evade their hunters completely, times when Oswald out-guessed him and he found a squadron of soldiers in his path, or was ambushed, or betrayed by an innkeeper or a ferryman; but a society with plenty of hounds and some modern technology was pitted against a psionic master with a medieval heart and a modern education. The lords didn't really understand how their gadgets worked, but Magnus did. He saw to it that they stopped working; he saw to it that the soldiers were looking the other way as he and Lord Aran crept by; he countered the ambushes with telekinesis reinforcing karate.

Siflot, meanwhile, found the children and brought them to Magnus and Lord Aran, and together they fought their way through seventy miles of patrols and sentries, of checkpoints and cordons, until finally the day came when they found the escaped serfs, or the serfs found them.

And so they came to Castlerock, and stood atop its highest pinnacle to look back over the way they had come, the free-lance and his apprentice, the lord and his little granddaughter, and the jester. How they got there is another tale, to be told in another time and another place; for now, all that matters is that they did come there, despite all the efforts of the lords and of Master Oswald and his team; and Lord Aran said to Magnus, "What comes now?"

Magnus shrugged. "You are the lord here, not I."

"I am the lord," Lord Aran rejoined, "but there is more to you than there seems." He peered keenly at his bodyguard. "You are not of this world, are you?"

Magnus stood very still for a moment, gazing out at the countryside.

Siflot looked up, more alert than alarmed.

Slowly, Magnus turned to the lord. "You have guessed it," he said, "and I should not be surprised. I knew you were acute, my lord."

"Thank you for the compliment," Lord Aran said, with only a trace of sarcasm. "May I know your true name, and station?"

"I am a knight," Magnus said slowly, "and heir to a lord."

Siflot stared, wide-eyed.

Lord Aran nodded, triumph in his gaze. "I knew it! Breeding cannot be hidden long, especially in such crises as we have weathered together, young man. What is your house and nation?"

"I am a d'Armand, of Maxima," Magnus said slowly, "though I grew up far from there."

Lord Aran nodded. "And how have you come to be here?"

"That, I am not at liberty to say," Magnus answered, "though I will tell Your Lordship that my spaceship awaits in orbit."

"And will you leave us, then?"

Ian looked up, alarmed.

"I fear I must," Magnus said, "for to aid you further would be to betray my comrades."

"Have you not betrayed them already, in aiding me?"

"They believe so," Magnus said, "but I know otherwise. They will find that their plans to help the people of this planet are advanced more than they could have hoped for in a single year, and will find that they merely need shift their strategy to incorporate the fact of your survival, and coming to Castlerock."

"Indeed!" the old lord said, with some asperity. "Then it was not loyalty alone, or friendship, that bade you save myself and my granddaughter."

"It was," Magnus contradicted, "but I had need

also to find a way to salvage the plans of my . . . friends, by saving you."

"Resolving a conflict of loyalties? Magnificent, if you achieved it! But how?"

"Yes, this is really quite interesting," Siflot said, composing himself to listen. "How shall Lord Aran survive, and Castlerock with him, without disrupting the plans of . . . our friends?"

"Why, by his own action," Magnus said. "I shall leave you a transceiver, with which His Lordship can access a transponder that will beam his voice to Terra. By that, he can declare Castlerock to be a sovereign nation, desiring associate membership in the Decentralized Democratic Tribunal, and asking its aid."

"But the D.D.T. will never interfere in the internal affairs of a planet!" Siflot protested.

Lord Aran glanced at him keenly, and Magnus, with a sense of satisfaction, knew that the old lord would not lack good advice. "It may, when that planet is not a member of the Tribunal, but is one the D.D.T. wishes to count among its members."

"But SCE—" Siflot coughed, then said, "Our friends would never allow it!"

"No, it would take the situation out of their control, wouldn't it?" Magnus smiled. "So they will, of course, intercept the message, and offer to give Castlerock support in their own right." He turned back to Lord Aran. "They will give you weapons, my lord, and instruction in their use, enough for you to be able to withstand the siege of the other lords."

"My fellow noblemen will hire off-planet aid," Lord Aran rumbled.

"They'll try," Magnus agreed, "but I think you will find that none will be willing to work for them, or sell them weapons."

"You, however, will find them quite willing, these off-planet men," Siflot suggested.

Lord Aran looked at him in surprise, and Magnus smiled. "Your enemies will not give up easily, though, my lord. It may be twenty years or more before they accept your dominion here as a fact they cannot change, and begin to ignore you. Even then, they will mount the occasional assault."

"If I have the resources they have, I can withstand them," Lord Aran rejoined. "But you assume these Castlerock folk, these stalwart gentlemen and freedmen, will accept me as their lord. You forget they have worked out their own council for governance."

"I do not doubt it, but I think you will find them turning to you for guidance more and more as the months pass. Certainly they will countenance your soliciting of off-planet help—and when they learn that the price of peace is for them to accept yourself, and your granddaughter after you, as their nominal lords, they will do so."

"The price of peace?" The old lord frowned.

"Of course, my lord," Siflot said softly. "If Castlerock is nominally your demesne, and the people on it not outlaws, but your serfs and gentry—why, then, your rival lords have an excuse to ignore it, a means of pretending that the status quo has been preserved, and that you have been punished sufficiently by ostracism from your own kind. In brief, if the Council accepts you as their President or some such, the other lords will have a means of saving face without continuing the war."

And SCENT, Magnus realized, would have its nucleus of democracy, and its beacon of hope for all the other serfs of Taxhaven.

But Lord Aran was staring at Siflot. "You are rather wise, for a fool. But of course—for you, too, are from off-planet, are you not? Tell me, what is *your* rank and station?"

"Alas! I am no lord, but only the son of a politican of gentle birth—with whose policies I could not agree."

"Which makes him the equivalent of a lord's heir, in terms of the Terran Sphere today," Magnus told Lord Aran.

But Siflot shook his head. "Not a lord! I was not born to a title."

"But a gentleman, certainly," Magnus insisted, "though I think you will find that such distinctions lack their accustomed force, my lord—on Castlerock."

"Perhaps it is just as well." The old lord sighed. "But you, Captain Pike—can you not stay with us as well?"

"I fear not, for although my friends may find excuses for Siflot's presence here, they cannot excuse my direct disobedience, my defiance of their orders. They must court-martial me, or forfeit all claim to authority and discipline. If I stay, they will find that they must besiege Castlerock to make of you the martyr they originally thought you would be. If I go, they will find excuses to support you." He smiled at the old lord. "So my duty to you, is to leave."

Ian gave an inarticulate cry.

"I know, lad." Magnus stepped forward to rest a hand on the boy's shoulder. "Would that I could take you with me—but your place is here. You are among your own kind, now—escaped serfs—and will find that your fellows hold you in high esteem."

"Escaped serf?" Lord Aran looked up. "He is not, then, a . . . gentleman's informal son?"

"He is no bastard, no, but a serf legitimately born," Magnus said. "Ian, tell him why you fled."

Ian swallowed, but faced the old lord bravely. "My lord was Lord Murthren, sir, and he sought to take my sister by force. My father found a way for her to escape to the forest—but for doing so, Lord Murthren had him flogged within an inch of his life. He knew that it would go hard with me for being his son, so with his last breath, or nearly, he bade me escape." Tears rolled down Ian's cheeks, but he stood staunchly and ignored them. "I fled to the green-wood, and was lucky enough to evade the hunters till my master, Captain Pike, took me under his care."

"The hunters! Then you are the lad who went into the Sacred Place!"

"I—I am, sir." Ian looked frightened, and Siflot moved to clasp the lad's shoulder in reassurance.

"But how is this?" Lord Aran frowned at Magnus. "Those shelters are keyed to admit only those who have the genetic pattern of the original founders!"

"Those founders were scarcely miserly about their genes, my lord," Magnus said grimly, "and their descendants were quite profligate with them. I think you will find that there are very few serfs who *cannot* be admitted to the Safety Bases if they wish it. Why else would Lord Murthren be so concerned about enforcing the taboo against their use?"

"A fascinating notion." Lord Aran turned to Ian. "And if you have noble blood in you, lad, you have some claim to gentility—indeed, I would say you have proved that claim, in your warding of the Lady Heloise. Nay, you shall be of my household and retinue now—my squire, and the Lady Heloise's bodyguard. Will you accept such service?"

"A—a squire?" Ian's eyes were huge and round. "To *you*, my lord? Oh, yes!"

"Oh, how wonderful, Ian!" Lady Heloise clapped her hands. "You will always be by us now!"

How easily the boy was impressed with even so minor a title as "squire"! Magnus reflected sourly that the people of this planet were indeed far from being ready for democracy.

The ferryman rowed him ashore in the hour before sunrise, his oars feathered in case of ambush. Magnus thanked him and stepped ashore, wrapped in a dark cloak. It was rough homespun, serf-made from the wool of the sheep who grazed the interior of the twenty-mile-long island, but it was warm, and dark enough to hide him.

Magnus strode up to the center of the beach and

thought the command, *Herkimer. Come pick me up now.*

Coming, Magnus, the voice answered inside his mind.

It would take some time, Magnus knew, even though Herkimer had stayed in geostationary orbit above wherever Magnus happened to be at the moment. Twenty thousand miles does take time to traverse, even if it's straight down. He composed himself to wait, and looked around for a boulder to sit on.

She stepped forth from among the rocks, in her own skin-fitting garb again, a body stocking of electric blue, covered by a golden vest with stiffened shoulders that tapered to cover her hips. Her hair was a golden cloud, loosed to catch and hold; her eyes were huge and so dark as to seem almost purple in the false dawn.

Magnus felt the old, familiar thrilling throughout his whole body, felt the wrenching within—and felt the automatic closing of his emotional armor as he gazed at her.

"So," she said as she came up to him, "you have won." She bowed her head, her face solemn, looking up at him through long lashes.

So it was to be seduction today, Magnus reflected wryly. When last they had met, it had been rage. "Perhaps," he said, "but you have, too."

"Oh yes, we have. We realized that almost as soon as your boat touched the island—that with Lord Aran there, we had a nucleus of democracy. By itself, it was doomed—and if it had survived, it could have only been a dictatorship. But with a lord there, and one who is a hero to all the serfs, there is the basis for the restraints of tradition, and a functioning constitution could emerge, complete with recognition of human rights."

"It could," Magnus alllowed, "with careful guidance."

"Yes, guidance. So we must support Castlerock, mustn't we? Make sure that they can hold off the lords, insinuate the notion that they can be recognized as just one more ducal fief so that the peers can overlook their existence—and advise and guide them, and through them, the rest of the planet."

Magnus nodded. "It should work out quite well."

"Yes, it should—and since Siflot is already established there, we'll have to overlook his peccadillo in helping you and Lord Aran, give him credit for having worked his way into the confidence of a group we need to influence, and restore him to good standing in the team."

Magnus nodded. "That would be the prudent course."

"Yes, wouldn't it?" Allouene said, with some irony. "You planned it this way all along, didn't you?"

"No, not really," Magnus said. "I only knew that Lord Aran was too good a human being to let die, and that the ideals he represented had to be preserved. I worked out the rest of it after the fact, while we were on the run. In fact, I didn't realize how to bring it all together, until we were safe on Castlerock."

"But once there, you took the final steps to make

sure we'd have to support them." For a moment, bitterness showed; then Allouene was all demure sweetness again. "We were honored to have you with us, Magnus."

Magnus stood frozen, letting the surge of emotion wash over him and recede. "So. You uncovered my true identity."

"Yes. Something you said during our last . . . conversation . . . made me realize that you didn't sound like the raw recruit you pretended to be."

Magnus shrugged. "I was. I learned a great deal in training."

"Yes, but you already knew a lot more. We checked the registration on your ship, found out it was brand-new and from Maxima, made by d'Armand Automatons, and that showed us where to look. We asked, and your relatives were glad to tell us what a wonderful young man you were, how helpful you had been, but no, you weren't part of the household, just a relative from a frontier planet, but that you couldn't tell them its name or location, because it was secret. That rang bells, and we checked the files under d'Armand. You might have told me you were the son of one of our most illustrious agents."

Magnus felt the stab of mingled pride and resentment that went with the recognition of his father's status. "I hadn't known Rodney d'Armand ranked so highly in the regard of his peers."

"Oh, he does, you may be sure! To turn a whole planet toward democracy, without having to send for a backup team? And to keep it that way, against the coordinated efforts of two extremely sophisticated enemy organizations, with almost no assistance except what he could raise locally? You *bet* he's famous!"

Magnus could have wished she had used some term other than "raised." "Then you can understand why I wish to be known for my own accomplishments, rather than for my father's."

She softened considerably—perhaps too much. "Yes, I can understand that. But the long and the short of it is, you grew up learning how to engineer social change, didn't you?"

Magnus shrugged impatiently. "I suppose I did, but I wasn't aware of it. It was in the air about me, in the food I ate—or at least, the conversations at table. But yes, you're right—once you had taught me the basics that Father never thought to state outright, once I began to try to work out such a puzzle for myself, it seemed to come naturally."

"And you're an esper, aren't you? A telepath and telekinetic, and everything else?"

"Not quite. I'm not a clairvoyant."

"Oh, yes, but you *are* everything else! You've known what I was thinking all along, haven't you?"

"No." Magnus shook his head emphatically. "We don't do that. It's the cornerstone of our ethics. We don't eavesdrop on other people's minds—unless they're enemies, or there's some other damn good reason." He thought of his cousin the professor with a pang.

Alloune stepped closer to him, very close, arms down at her sides, frowning a little, peering up into his face. Magnus stood braced, though his body seemed to thrum with the nearness of hers.

"You can tell what I'm thinking right now, can't you?" she said.

Magnus's face broke into a sharp smile, amused. "Yes, but it doesn't take telepathy."

She stared at him, paling, then turned away, flushing. "I thought you were attracted to me . . . Magnus. When we first met."

"And every time I've talked to you since," Magnus said softly. "Oh yes, I've been attracted, painfully attracted—and you didn't just think it, you knew it."

She turned back to him with a lazy smile of amusement, eyes half-lidded. "Yes, and it was wonderful. Every woman wants to feel wanted. I was quite flattered—really."

"Why, thank you." Magnus inclined his head gravely.

"Oh, can't you stop that?" she cried. "Can't you drop your guard, just for an instant? Can't you talk to me as man to woman for a little while?"

"Why, of course." But for a fleeting instant, Magnus wondered if he still could. "However, if I did, could you talk to me without thinking of me as a potential asset? Could you talk to me without being aware of how I could help you, be useful to you? Could you talk to me as just Gar Pike, forgetting that I'm Magnus d'Armand?"

"Of course I couldn't!" she cried. "Could you talk to me without being aware of my body, my face, my hair? What you can do, who your father was, they're as much a part of you as my beauty is a part of me!

Can you talk to me without being aware of what I can do for you?"

"Of course," Magnus said, "beyond the immediate and personal."

"Oh, so sex isn't part of what I can do for you!"

"I would be quite content," Magnus assured her, "if sex was the only thing you wanted of me."

"It's not the same!"

"I think it is," Magnus said, "but even if it is not, it is certainly analogous."

"Must you be so damn formal!" she cried, clenching her fists.

"Yes," Magnus said, "I must. You know I must."

She glared at him, outraged, then remembered herself and dropped her gaze, forcing her fists to unclench, her emotions to smooth out. Finally, she looked up at him with a smile that held some fraction of her usual allure. "All right. If I do what you want, will you do what I want?"

"No," he said. "That would be wrong now."

"But *why*!"

He gazed down at her for the space of ten heartbeats while she glared back up, and he debated whether he should say it or not, whether it would hurt her or not, then decided that it would hurt right now, but help her later.

"Because," he said, "it would need love."

She stared at him, her face slowly blanching, then finally looked down, but he could tell from the set of her shoulders how enraged she was.

"At least do me this much," she said, her voice low and strained, not looking at him. "If you won't help me, at least don't louse things up for me. All right?"

"Certainly." Magnus inclined his head. "I will go."

She looked up, startled by the ease of her victory. "Go? Where?"

Magnus shrugged impatiently. "Wherever the mood takes me."

"Of course," she whispered. "You can, can't you? You're rich."

Magnus didn't disillusion her. After all, he was rich, in a fashion—he could make gold whenever he wanted to, or diamonds.

"I'll tell them to watch out for you," she said softly.

"Thank you." Magnus bowed again. "That tells me where *not* to go."

She smiled, amused for a second, solacing herself with a small victory. "I don't believe you."

Magnus gave her a real smile in return. "You're wise."

They stood a moment in silence, as the sun painted the sky in voluptuous tones behind her. Then finally she whispered, "Will you ever come back?"

Magnus shrugged. "I doubt it—but I'm not promising anything."

"Of course you wouldn't," she said, with irony. Then she pulled herself together, turned the soulful eyes on him, and made one last try. "I could have loved you, Magnus—but I'm hurt, I'm so terribly hurt, by your turning against me."

He realized the name of the game, the theatrical aspect of it, and gave her the solace she was asking for. "Forgive me."

"I might." She looked up at him through long lashes again. "I could love you again, even now—if you could join with me once more, and help me undo the damage you've done."

Magnus tried to look anguished. "But what about the people? What about the sufferings of the ones who are alive today? Of their children? Their children's children?"

She stared—this wasn't what she had been expecting—but she said, mournfully, "We have to learn who we can help and who we can't, Magnus, and be content with doing what little we can that will someday result in everyone being free."

"But I cannot stand by and watch others suffer. I lack the self-discipline." Magnus smiled sadly for her. "I could have loved you mightily, Allouene—but the good of the people has come between us."

She held still for a moment, staring, her eyes growing large. Then she said, her voice husky, "Promise it to me, after all—promise you won't come back."

He bowed his head. "As you wish. Yes. I owe you that much."

And the great golden ship fell down from the sky.

After he was aboard, after they had hovered over Castlerock and dropped a parachute with a transceiver into Siflot's waiting hands, after the hatch had closed safely behind him again, he turned away to collapse into his acceleration couch and let the de-

spair overwhelm him for a few minutes—
overwhelm, and recede, and dwindle. Then he could
think once again, and reflect in bitterness that love
had once more passed him by, that Cupid had once
again led him to a woman who was far more interested in using him than in loving him. He began to
suspect that the Archer had a grudge against him,
that True Love might be the reality for some, but
would probably prove only a myth for him.

Finally, he roused himself, sitting up a little
straighter and telling Herkimer, "Prepare to leave orbit."

"Prepared," the robot confirmed. "Where would
you like to go, Magnus?"

Magnus waved a hand. "Oh, someplace interesting. Look through your files and see what you can
find."

"What parameters shall I look for, Magnus?"

"Oppressed peasants." Magnus's voice took on
strength and conviction again. "Dissipated, tyranni-
cal lords. Leaders who recruited a bunch of ordinary
people and went off with them to try to build their
own private kingdoms. Someplace where my life
might do some good."

"Searching."

So was Magnus.